Randall Garrett

Pagan Passions
(Unabridged)

OK Publishing 2021

Randall Garrett
Pagan Passions

(Unabridged)

Published by
MUSAICUM
Books

- Advanced Digital Solutions & High-Quality book Formatting -

musaicumbooks@okpublishing.info

2021 OK Publishing

ISBN 978-80-272-7972-2

Contents

CHAPTER 1

The girl came toward him across the silent room. She was young. She was beautiful. Her red hair curled like a flame round her eager, heart-shaped face. Her arms reached for him. Her hands touched him. Her eyes were alive with the light of pure love. I am yours, the eyes kept saying. Do with me as you will.

Forrester watched the eyes with a kind of fascination.

Now the girl's mouth opened, the lips parted slightly, and her husky voice murmured softly: "Take me. Take me."

Forrester blinked and stepped back.

"My God," he said. "This is ridiculous."

The girl pressed herself against him. The sensation was, Forrester thought with a kind of awe, undeniably pleasant. He tried to remember the girl's name, and couldn't. She wriggled slightly and her arms went up around him. Her hands clasped at the back of his neck and her mouth moved, close to his ear.

"Please," she whispered. "I want you...."

Forrester felt his head swimming. He opened his mouth but nothing whatever came out. He shut his mouth and tried to think what to do with his hands. They were hanging foolishly at his sides. The girl came even closer, something Forrester would have thought impossible.

Time stopped. Forrester swam in a pink haze of sensations. Only one small corner of his brain refused to lose itself in the magnificence of the moment. In that corner, Forrester felt feverishly uncomfortable. He tried again to remember the girl's name, and failed again. Of course, there was really no reason why he should have known the name. It was, after all, only the first day of class.

"Please," he said valiantly. "Miss —"

He stopped.

"I'm Maya Wilson," the girl said in his ear. "I'm in your class, Mr. Forrester. Introductory World History." She bit his ear gently. Forrester jumped.

None of the textbooks of propriety he had ever seen seemed to cover the situation he found himself in. What did one do when assaulted (pleasantly, to be sure, but assault was assault) by a lovely girl who happened to be one of your freshman students? She had called him Mr. Forrester. That was right and proper, even if it was a little silly. But what should he call her? Miss Wilson?

That didn't sound right at all. But, for other reasons, Maya sounded even worse.

The girl said: "Please," and added to the force of the word with another little wriggle against Forrester. It solved his problems. There was now only one thing to do, and he did it.

He broke away, found himself on the other side of his desk, looking across at an eager, wet-lipped freshman student.

"Well," he said. There was a lone little bead of sweat trickling down his forehead, across his frontal ridge and down one cheek. He ignored it bravely, trying to think what to do next. "Well," he repeated at last, in what he hoped was a gentle and fatherly tone. "Well, well, well, well, well." It didn't seem to have any effect. Perhaps, he thought, an attempt to put things back on the teacher-student level might have better results. "You wanted me to see you?" he said in a grave, scholarly tone. Then, gulping briefly, he amended it in a voice that had suddenly grown an octave: "You wanted to see me? I mean, you —"

"Oh," Maya Wilson said. "Oh, my goodness, *yes*, Mr. Forrester!"

She made a sudden sensuous motion that looked to Forrester as if she had suddenly abolished bones. But it wasn't unpleasant. Far from it. Quite the contrary.

Forrester licked his lips, which were suddenly very dry. "Well," he said. "What about, Miss-uh-Miss Wilson?"

"Please call me Maya, Mr. Forrester. And I'll call you —" There was a second of hesitation. "Mr. Forrester," Maya said plaintively, "what is your first name?"

"First name?" Forrester tried to think of his first name. "You want to know my first name?"

"Well," Maya said, "I want to call you something. Because after all —" She looked as if she were going to leap over the desk.

"You may call me," Forrester said, grasping at his sanity, "Mr. Forrester."

Maya sidled around the desk quietly. "Mr. Forrester," she said, reaching for him, "I wanted to talk to you about the Introductory World History course."

Forrester shivered as if someone had thrown cold water on his rising aspirations.

"Oh," he said.

"That's right," Maya whispered. Her mouth was close to his ear again. Other parts of her were close to other parts of him once more. Forrester found it difficult to concentrate.

"I've *got* to pass the course, Mr. Forrester," Maya whispered. "I've just *got* to."

Somehow, Forrester retained just enough control of his faculties to remember the standard answer to protestations like that one. "Well, I'm sure you will," he said in what he hoped was a calm, hearty, hopeful voice. He was reasonably sure it wasn't any of those, and even surer that it wasn't all three. "You seem like a —like a fairly intelligent young lady," he finished lamely.

"Oh, no," she said. "I'm sure I won't be able to remember all those old-fashioned dates and things. Never. Never." Suddenly she pressed herself wildly against him, throwing him slightly off balance. Locked together, the couple reeled against the desk. Forrester felt it digging into the small of his back. "I'll do anything to pass the course, Mr. Forrester!" she vowed. "Anything!"

The insistent pressure of the desk top robbed the moment of some of its natural splendor. Forrester disengaged himself gently and slid a little out of the way. "Now, now," he said, moving rapidly across the room toward a blank wall. "This sort of thing isn't usually done, Maya. I mean, Miss Wilson. I mean —"

"But —"

"People just don't do such things," Forrester said sternly. He thought of escaping through the door, but the picture that arose immediately in his mind dissuaded him. He saw Maya pursuing him passionately through the halls while admiring students and faculty stared after them. "Anyhow," he added as an afterthought, "not at the *beginning* of the semester."

"Oh," Maya said. She was advancing on him slowly. "You mean, I ought to see if I can pass the course on my own first, and *then* —"

"Not at all," Forrester cut in.

Maya sniffed sadly. "Oh, you just don't understand," she said. "You're an Athenian, aren't you?"

"Athenan," Forrester said automatically. It was a correction he found himself called upon to make ten or twelve times a week. "An Athenian is a resident of Athens, while an Athenan is a worshipper of the Goddess Athena. We —"

"I understand," Maya said. "I suppose it's like us. We don't like to be called Aphrodisiacs, you know. We prefer Venerans."

She was leaning across the desk. Forrester, though he supposed some people might be fussy about it, could see no objection whatever to the term Aphrodisiacs. A wild thought dealing with Spheres of Influence strayed into his mind, and he suppressed it firmly.

The girl was a Veneran. A worshipper of Venus, Goddess of Love.

Her choice of religion, he thought, was unusually appropriate.

And as for his....

CHAPTER 2

It was hard to believe that, only an hour or so before, he had been peaceful and calm, entirely occupied with his duties in the great Temple of Pallas Athena. His mind gave a sudden, panic-stricken leap and he was back there again, standing at the rear of the vast room and focusing all of his strained attention on it.

The glowing embers in the golden incense tripods were dying now, but the heavy clouds of frankincense, still tingled with the sweet aroma of balsam and clove, hung heavily in the quiet air over the main altar. In the flickering illumination of the gas sconces around the walls, the figures on the great tapestries seemed to move with a subtle life of their own.

Even though the great brazen gong had sounded for the last time twenty minutes before, marking the end of the service, there were still a few worshippers in the pews, seated with heads bowed in prayer to the Goddess. Forrester considered them carefully: average-looking people, a sprinkling of youngsters, and in the far corner a girl who looked just a little like…

Forrester peered more closely. It wasn't just a slight resemblance; the girl really seemed to be Gerda Symes. Her long blonde hair shone in the dimness. Forrester couldn't see her very clearly, but his imagination was working overtime. Her magnificently curved figure, her wonderful face, her fiery personality were as much a part of his dreams as the bed he slept on.

If not for her brother…

Forrester sighed and forced himself to return his attention to his duties. His hands remained clasped reverently at his breast. Whatever battle went on in his mind, the remaining few people in the great room would see nothing but what was fitting. At any rate, he told himself, he made rather an imposing sight in his robes, and, with a stirring of vanity which he prayed Athena to chasten, he was rather proud of it.

He was a fairly tall man, just a shade under six feet, but his slight paunch made him seem shorter than he was. His face was round and smooth and pleasant, and that made him look younger than he was: twenty-one instead of twenty-seven. As befitted an acolyte of the Goddess of Wisdom, his dark, curly hair was cut rather long. When he bowed to a departing worshipper, lowering his head in graceful acknowledgment of their deferential nods, he felt that he made a striking and commanding picture.

Though, of course, the worshippers weren't doing him any honor. That bow was not for him, but directed toward the Owl, the symbol of the Goddess embroidered on the breast of the white tunic. As an acolyte, after all, he rated just barely above a layman; he had no powers whatever.

Athena knew that, naturally. But somehow it was a little difficult to get it through his own doubtless too-thick skull. He'd often dreamed of power. Being a priest or a priestess, for instance-now that meant something. At least people paid attention to you if you were a member of the hierarchy, favored of the Gods. But, Forrester knew, there was no chance of that any more. Either you were picked before you were twenty-one, or you weren't picked at all, and that was all there was to it. In spite of his looks, Forrester was six years past the limit.

And so he'd become an acolyte. Sometimes he wondered how much of that had been an honest desire to serve Athena, and how much a sop to his worldly vanity. Certainly a college history instructor had enough to do, without adding the unpaid religious services of an acolyte to his work.

But these were thoughts unworthy of his position. They reminded him of his own childhood, when he had dreamed of becoming one of the Lesser Gods, or even Zeus himself! Zeus had provided the best answer to those dreams, Forrester knew. "Now I am a man," Zeus had said, "and I put away childish things."

Well, Forrester considered, it behooved him to put away childish things, too. A mere vanity, a mere love of spectacle, was unworthy of the Goddess he served. And his costume and bearing certainly hadn't got him very far with Gerda.

He tore his eyes away from her again, and sighed.

Before he could bring his mind back to Athena, there was an interruption.

Another white-clad acolyte moved out of the shadows to his right and came softly toward him. "Forrester?" he whispered.

Forrester turned, recognizing young Bates, a chinless boy of perhaps twenty-two, with the wide, innocent eyes of the born fanatic. But it didn't become a servant of Athena to think ill of her other servants, Forrester reminded himself. Brushing the possibility of a rude reply from his mind, Forrester said simply: "Yes? What is it?"

"There's a couple of Temple Myrmidons to see you outside," Bates whispered. "I'll take over your post."

Forrester responded with no more than a simple nod, as if the occurrence were one that happened every day. But it was not only the thought of leaving Gerda that moved him. As he turned and strode to the small door that led to the side room off the main auditorium, he was thinking furiously under his calm exterior.

Temple Myrmidons! What could they want with him? As an acolyte, he was at least immune to arrest by the civil police, and even the Temple Myrmidons had no right to take him into custody without a warrant from the Pontifex himself.

But such a warrant was a serious affair. What had he done wrong?

He tried to think of some cause for an arrest. Blasphemy? Sacrilege? But he found nothing except his interior thoughts. And those, he told himself with a blaze of anger fierce enough to surprise him, were nobody's business but his own and Athena's. Authorities either less personal or more temporal had no business dealing with thoughts.

Beyond those, there wasn't a thing. No irreverence toward any of the Gods, in his private life, his religious functions or his teaching position, at least as far as he could recall. The Gods knew that unorthodoxy in an Introductory History course, for instance, was not only unwise but damned difficult.

Of course, he was aware of the real position of the Gods. They weren't omnipotent. Their place in the scheme of things was high, but they were certainly not equal with the One who had created the Universe and the Gods themselves in the first place. Possibly, Forrester had always thought, they could be equated with the indefinite "angels" of the religions that had been popular during his grandfather's time, sixty years ago, before the return of the Gods. But that was an uncertain theological notion, and Forrester was quite ready to abandon it in the face of good argument to the contrary.

Whatever they were, the Gods were certainly the Gods of Earth now.

The Omnipotent Creator had evidently left it for them to run, while he went about his own mysterious business, far from the understanding or the lives of men. The Gods, omnipotent or not, ran the world and everything in it.

And if, like Forrester, you knew that omnipotence wasn't their strong point, you just didn't mention it. It would have been impolite to have done so-like talking about sight to a blind man. And "impolite" was not the only word that covered the case. The Gods had enough power, as everyone knew, to avenge any blasphemies against them. And careless mention of limitations on their power would surely be construed as blasphemy, true or not.

Forrester had never even thought of doing such a thing.

So what, he thought, did the Temple Myrmidons want with him?

He came to the anteroom and went in, seeing the two of them at once. They were big, burly chaps with hard faces, and the pistols that were holstered at their sides looked completely unnecessary. Forrester took a deep breath and went a step forward. There he stopped, staring.

The Myrmidons were strangers to him-and now he understood why. Neither was wearing the shoulder-patch Owl of Minerva/Athena. Both proudly sported the Thunderbolt of Zeus/Jupiter, the All-Father himself.

Whatever it is, Forrester told himself with a sinking sensation, *it's serious.*

One of the Myrmidons looked him up and down in a casual, half-contemptuous way. "You're William Forrester?"

"That's right," Forrester said, knowing that he looked quite calm, and wondering, at the same time, whether or not he would live out the next few minutes. The Myrmidons of Zeus/Jupiter didn't come around to other temples on unimportant errands. "May I help you?" he went on, feeling foolish.

"Let's see your ID card, please," the Myrmidon said in the same tone as before. That puzzled Forrester. He doubted whether examination of credentials was a part of the routine preceding arrest-or execution, for that matter. The usual procedure was, and probably always had been, to act first and apologize later, if at all.

Maybe whatever he'd done had been so important they couldn't afford to make mistakes.

But did the Myrmidon really think that an imposter could parade around in an acolyte's tunic in the very Temple of Pallas Athena without being caught by one of the Athenan Myrmidons, or some other acolyte or priest?

Maybe a thing like that could happen in one of the other Temples, Forrester thought. But here at Pallas Athena people took the Goddess's attribute of wisdom seriously. What the Dionysians might do, he reflected, was impossible to say. Or, for that matter, the Venerans.

But he produced his identity card and handed it to the Myrmidon. It was compared with a card the Myrmidon dug out of his pouch, and the thumbprints on both cards were examined side by side.

After a while, Forrester got his card back.

The Myrmidon said: "We —" and began to cough.

His companion came over to slap him on the back with bone-crushing blows. Forrester watched without changing expression.

Some seconds passed.

Then the Myrmidon choked, swallowed, straightened and said, his face purple: "All this incense. Not like what we've got over at the All-Father's Temple. Enough to choke a man to death."

Forrester murmured politely.

"Back to business-right?" He favored Forrester with a rather savage-looking smile, and Forrester allowed his own lips to curve gently and respectfully upward.

It didn't look as if he *were* going to be killed, after all.

"Important instructions for you," the Myrmidon said. "From the Pontifex Maximus. And not to be repeated to any mortal-understand?"

Forrester nodded.

"And that means *any* mortal," the Myrmidon said. "Girl friend, wife-or don't you Athenans go in for that sort of thing? Now, up at the All-Father's Temple, we —"

His companion gave him a sharp dig in the ribs.

"Oh," the Myrmidon said. "Sure. Well. Instructions not to be repeated. Right?"

"Right," Forrester said.

Instructions? From the Pontifex Maximus? *Secret* instructions?

Forrester's mind spun dizzily. This was no arrest. This was something very special and unique. He tried once more to imagine what it was going to be, and gave it up in wonder.

The Myrmidon produced another card from his pouch. There was nothing on it but the golden Thunderbolt of the All-Father —but that was quite enough.

Forrester accepted the card dumbly.

"You will report to the Tower of Zeus at eighteen hundred hours exactly," the Myrmidon said. "Got that?"

"You mean today?" Forrester said, and cursed himself for sounding stupid. But the Myrmidon appeared not to have noticed.

"Today, sure," he said. "Eighteen hundred. Just present this card."

He stepped back, obviously getting ready to leave. Forrester watched him for one long second, and then burst out: "What do I do after that?"

"Just be a good boy. Do what you're told. Ask no questions. It's better that way."

Forrester thought of six separate replies and settled on a seventh. "All right," he said.

"And remember," the Myrmidon said, at the outside door, "don't mention this to anyone. *Not anyone!*"

The door banged shut.

Forrester found himself staring at the card he held. He put it away in his case, alongside the ID card. Then, dazed, he went on back to the acolyte's sacristy, took off his white tunic and put on his street clothes.

What did they want with him at the Tower of Zeus? It didn't really sound like an arrest. If it had been that, the Myrmidons themselves would have taken him.

So what did the Pontifex Maximus want with William Forrester?

He spent some time considering it, and then, taking a deep breath, he forced it out of his mind. He would know at eighteen hundred, and such were the ways of the Gods that he would not know one second before.

So there was no point in worrying about it, he told himself. He almost made himself believe it.

But wiping speculation out of his mind left an unwelcome and uneasy vacancy. Forrester replaced it with thought of the morning's service in the Temple. Such devotion was probably valuable, anyhow, in a spiritual sense. It brought him closer to the Gods....

The Gods he wanted desperately to be like.

That, he told himself sharply, was foolishness of the most senseless kind.

He blinked it away.

The Goddess Athena had appeared herself at the service-sufficient reason for thinking of it now. The statuesquely beautiful Goddess with her severely swept-back blonde hair and her deep gray eyes was the embodiment of the wisdom and strength for which her worshippers especially prayed. Her beauty was almost unworldly, impossible of existence in a world which contained mortals.

She reminded Forrester, ever so slightly (and, of course, in a reverent way), of Gerda Symes.

There seemed to be a great many forbidden thoughts floating around this day. Resolutely, Forrester went back to thinking about the morning's service.

The Goddess had appeared only long enough to impart her blessing, but her calm, beautifully controlled contralto voice had brought a sense of peace to everyone in the auditorium. To be doggedly practical, there was no way of knowing whether the Goddess's presence was an appearance-in person, or an "appearance" by Divine Vision. But that really didn't matter. The effect was always just the same.

Forrester went on out the front portals of the Temple of Wisdom and down the long, wide steps onto Fifth Avenue. He paid homage with a passing glance to the great Owls flanking the entrance. Symbolic of Athena, they had replaced the stone lions which had formerly stood there.

The street was busy with hurrying crowds, enlivened here and there by Temple Myrmidons-from the All-Father, from Bacchus, from Venus-even one from Pallas Athena herself, a broad-beamed swaggerer whom Forrester knew and disliked. The man came striding up the steps, greeted Forrester with a bare nod, and disappeared at top speed into the Temple.

Forrester sighed and glanced south, down toward 34th Street, where the huge Tower of Zeus, a hundred and four stories high, loomed over all the other buildings in the city.

At eighteen hundred he would be in that tower-for what purpose, he had no idea.

Well, that was in the future, and he...

A voice said: "Well! Hello, Bill!"

Forrester turned, knowing exactly what to expect, and disliking it in advance. The bluff over-heartiness of the voice was matched by the gross and hairy figure that confronted him. In some disarray, and managing to look as if he needed simultaneously a bath, a shave, a disinfecting and a purgative, the figure approached Forrester with a rolling walk that was too flat-footed for anything except an elephant.

"How's the Owl-boy today?" said the voice, and the body stuck out a flabby, hairy white hand.

Forrester winced. "I'm fine," he said evenly. "And how's the winebibber?"

"Good for you," the figure said. "A little wine for your Stomach's sake, as good old Bacchus always says. Only we make it a lot, eh?" He winked and nudged Forrester in the ribs.

"Sure, sure," Forrester said. He wished desperately that he could take the gross fool and tear him into tastefully arranged pieces. But there was always Gerda. And since this particular idiot happened to be her younger brother, Ed Symes, anything in the nature of violence was unthinkable.

Gerda's opinion of her brother was touching, reverent, and-Forrester thought savagely-not in the least borne out by any discoverable facts.

And a worshipper of Bacchus! Not that Forrester had anything against the orgiastic rites indulged in by the Dionysians, the Panites, the Apollones or even the worst and wildest of them all, the Venerans. If that was how the Gods wanted to be worshipped, then that was how they should be worshipped.

And, as a matter of fact, it sounded like fun-if, Forrester considered, entirely too public for his taste.

If he preferred the quieter rites of Athena, or of Juno, Diana or Ceres-and even Ceresians became a little wild during the spring fertility rites, especially in the country, where the farmers depended on her for successful crops-well, that was no more than a personal preference.

But the idea of Ed Symes involved in a Bacchic orgy was just a little too much for the normal mind, or the normal stomach.

"Hey," Ed said suddenly. "Where's Gerda? Still in the Temple?"

"I didn't see her," Forrester said. There *had* been a woman who'd looked like her. But that hadn't been Gerda. *She'd* have waited for him here.

And —

"Funny," Ed said.

"Why?" Forrester said. "I didn't see her. I don't think she attended the service this morning, that's all."

He wanted very badly to hit Symes. Just once. But he knew he couldn't.

First of all, there was Gerda. And then, as an acolyte, he was proscribed by law from brawling. No one would hit an acolyte; and if the acolyte were built like Forrester, striking another man might be the equivalent of murder. One good blow from Forrester's fist might break the average man's jaw.

That was, he discovered, a surprisingly pleasant thought. But he made himself keep still as the fat fool went on.

"Funny she didn't attend," Symes said. "But maybe she's gotten wise to herself. There was a celebration up at the Temple of Pan in Central Park, starting at midnight, and going on through the morning. Spring Rites. Maybe she went there."

"I doubt it," Forrester said instantly. "That's hardly her type of worship."

"Isn't it?" Symes said.

"It doesn't fit her. That kind of —"

"I know. Gerda's like you. A little stuffy."

"It's not being stuffy," Forrester started to explain. "It's —"

"Sure," Symes said. "Only she's not as much of a prude as you are. I couldn't stand her if she were."

"On the other hand, she's not a —"

"Not an Owl-boy of Owl-boys like you."

"Not a drunken blockhead," Forrester finished triumphantly. "At least she's got a decent respect for wisdom and learning."

Symes stepped back, a movement for which Forrester felt grateful. No matter how far away Ed Symes was, he was still too close.

"Who you calling a blockhead, buster?" Symes said. His eyes narrowed to piggish little slits.

Forrester took a deep breath and reminded himself not to hit the other man. "You," he said, almost mildly. "If brains were radium, you couldn't make a flicker on a scintillation counter."

It was just a little doubtful that Symes understood the insult. But he obviously knew it had been one. His face changed color to a kind of grayish purple, and his hands clenched slowly at his sides. Forrester stood watching him quietly.

Symes made a sound like *Rrr* and took a breath. "If you weren't an acolyte, I'd take a poke at you just to see you bounce."

"Sure you would," Forrester agreed politely.

Symes went *Rrr* again and there was a longer silence. Then he said: "Not that I'd hit you anyhow, buster. It'd go against my grain. Not the acolyte business-if you didn't look so much like Bacchus, I'd take the chance."

Forrester's jaw ached. In a second he realized why; he was clenching his teeth tightly. Perhaps it was true that he did look a little like Bacchus, but not enough for Ed Symes to kid about it.

Symes grinned at him. Symes undoubtedly thought the grin gave him a pleasant and carefree expression. It didn't. "Suppose I go have a look for Gerda myself," he said casually, heading up the stairs toward the temple entrance. "After all, you're so busy looking at books, you might have missed her."

And what, Forrester asked himself, was the answer to that-except a punch in the mouth?

It really didn't matter, anyhow. Symes was on his way into the temple, and Forrester could just ignore him.

But, damn it, why did he let the young idiot get his goat that way? Didn't he have enough self-control just to ignore Symes and his oafish insults?

Forrester supposed sadly that he didn't. Oh, well, it just made another quality he had to pray to Athena for.

Then he glanced at his wristwatch and stopped thinking about Symes entirely.

It was twelve-forty-five. He had to be at work at thirteen hundred.

Still angry, underneath the sudden need for speed, he turned and sprinted toward the subway.

"And thus," Forrester said tiredly, "having attempted to make himself the equal of the Gods, Man was given a punishment befitting such arrogance." He paused and took a breath, surveying the twenty-odd students in the classroom (and some, he told himself wryly, *very* odd) with a sort of benign boredom.

History I, Introductory Survey of World History, was a simple enough course to teach, but its very simplicity was its undoing, Forrester thought. The deadly dullness of the day-after-day routine was enough to wear out the strongest soul.

Freshmen, too, seemed to get stupider every year. Certainly, when *he'd* been seventeen, he'd been different altogether. Studious, earnest, questioning...

Then he stopped himself and grinned. He'd probably seemed even worse to his own instructors.

Where had he been? Slowly, he picked up the thread. There was a young blonde girl watching him eagerly from a front seat. What was her name? Forrester tried to recall it and couldn't. Well, this was only the first day of term. He'd get to know them all soon enough-well enough, anyhow, to dislike most of them.

But the eager expression on the girl's face unnerved him a little. The rest of the class wasn't paying anything like such strict attention. As a matter of fact, Forrester suspected two young boys in the back of being in a trance.

Well, he could stop that. But...

She was really quite attractive, Forrester told himself. Of course, she was nothing but a fresh, pretty, eager seventeen-year-old, with a figure that...

She was, Forrester reminded himself sternly, a student.

And he was supposed to be an instructor.

18

He cleared his throat. "Man went hog-wild with his new-found freedom from divine guidance," he said. "Woman did, too, as a matter of fact."

Now what unholy devil had made him say that? It wasn't a part of the normal lecture for first day of the new term. It was-well, it was just a little risqué for students. Some of their parents might complain, and…

But the girl in the front row was smiling appreciatively. *I wonder what she's doing in an Introductory course*, Forrester thought, leaping with no evidence at all to the conclusion that the girl's mind was much too fine and educated to be subjected to the general run of classes. *Private tutoring* …he began, and then cut himself off sharply, found his place in the lecture again and went on:

"When the Gods decided to sit back and observe for a few thousand years, they allowed Man to go his merry way, just to teach him a lesson."

The boys in the back of the room were definitely in a trance.

Forrester sighed. "And the inevitable happened," he said. "From the eighth century b.c., Old Style, until the year 1971 a.d., Old Style, Man's lot went from bad to worse. Without the Gods to guide him he bred bigger and bigger wars and greater and greater empires-beginning with the conquests of the mad Alexander of Macedonia and culminating in the opposing Soviet and American Spheres of Influence during the last century."

Spheres of Influence….

Forrester's gaze fell on the blonde girl again. She certainly had a well-developed figure. And she did seem so eager and attentive. He smiled at her tentatively. She smiled back.

"Urg …" he said aloud.

The class didn't seem to notice. That, Forrester told himself sourly, was probably because they weren't listening.

He swallowed, wrenched his gaze from the girl, and said: "The Soviet-American standoff-for that is what it was-would most probably have resulted in the destruction of the human race." It had no effect on the class. The destruction of the human race interested nobody. "However," Forrester said gamely, "this form of insanity was too much for the Gods to allow. They therefore —"

The bell rang, signifying the end of the period. Forrester didn't know whether to feel relieved or annoyed.

"All right," he said. "That's all for today. Your first assignment will be to read and carefully study Chapters One and Two of the textbook."

Silence gave way to a clatter of noise as the students began to file out. Forrester saw the front-row blonde rise slowly and gracefully. Any doubts he might have entertained (that is, he told himself wryly, any *entertaining* doubts) about her figure were resolved magnificently. He felt a little sweat on the palm of his hands, told himself that he was being silly, and then answered himself that the hell he was.

The blonde gave him a slow, sweet smile. The smile promised a good deal more than Forrester thought likely of fulfillment.

He smiled back.

It would have been impolite, he assured himself, not to have done so.

The girl left the room, and a remaining crowd of students hurried out after her. The crowd included two blinking boys, awakened by the bell from what had certainly been a trance. Forrester made a mental note to inquire after their records and to speak with the boys himself when he got the chance.

No sense in disturbing a whole class to discipline them.

He stacked his papers carefully, taking a good long time about it in order to relax himself and let his palms dry. His mind drifted back to the blonde, and he reined it in with an effort and let it go exploring again on safer ground. The class itself …actually, he thought, he rather liked teaching. In spite of the petty irritations that came from driving necessary knowledge into the heads of stubbornly unwilling students, it was a satisfying and important job. And, of course, it was an honor to hold the position he did. Ever since it had been revealed that the goddess Columbia was another manifestation of Pallas Athena herself, the University had grown tremendously in stature.

And after all...

Whistling faintly behind his teeth, Forrester zipped up his filled briefcase and went out into the hall. He ignored the masses of students swirling back and forth in the corridors, and, finding a stairway, went up to his second-floor office.

He fumbled for his key, found it, and opened the ground-glass door.

Then, stepping in, he came to a full stop.

The girl had been waiting for him-Maya Wilson.

———————————————

And now here she was, talking about the Goddess of Love. Forrester gulped.

"Anyhow," he said at random, "I'm an Athenan." He remembered that he had already said that. Did it matter? "But what does all this have to do with your passing, or not passing, the course?" he went on.

"Oh," Maya said. "Well, I prayed to Aphrodite for help in passing the course. And the Temple Priestess told me I'd have to make a sacrifice to the Goddess. In a way."

"A sacrifice?" Forrester gulped. "You mean —"

"Not the First Sacrifice," she laughed. "That was done with solemn ceremonies when I was seventeen."

"Now, wait a minute —"

"Please," Maya said. "Won't you listen to me?"

Forrester looked at her limpid blue eyes and her lovely face. "Sure. Sorry."

"Well, then, it's like this. If a person loves a subject, it's that much easier to understand it. And the Goddess has promised me that if I love the instructor, I'll love the subject. It's like sympathetic magic-see?"

Her explanation was so brisk and simple that Forrester recoiled. "Hold on," he said. "Just hold your horses. Do you mean you're in love with me?"

Maya smiled. "I think so," she said, and very suddenly she was on Forrester's side of the desk, pressing up against him. Her hand caressed the back of his neck and her fingers tangled in his hair. "Kiss me and let's find out."

CHAPTER 3

Resistance, such as it was, crumbled in a hurry. Forrester complied with fervor. An endless time went by, punctuated only by short breaths between the kisses. Forrester's hands began to rove. So did Maya's.

She began to unbutton his shirt.

Not to be outdone, his own fingers got busy with buttons, zippers, hooks and the other temporary fastenings with which female clothing is encumbered. He was swimming in a red sea of passion and the Egyptians were nowhere in sight. Absently, he got an arm out of his shirt, and at the same time somehow managed to undo the final button of a series. Maya's blouse fell free.

Forrester felt like stout Cortez.

He pulled the girl to him, feeling the surprisingly cool touch of her flesh against his. Under the blouse and skirt, he was discovering, she wore very little, and that was just as well; nagging thoughts about the doubtful privacy of his office were beginning to assail him.

Nevertheless, he persevered. Maya was as eager as he had ever dreamed of being, and their embrace reached a height of passion and began to climb and climb to hitherto unknown peaks of sensation.

Forrester was busy for some time discovering things he had never known, and a lot of things he had known before, but never so well. Every motion was met with a reaction that was more than equal and opposite, every sensation unlocked the doors to whole galleries of new sensations. Higher and higher went his emotional thermometer, higher and higher and higher and higher and ...

Very suddenly, he discovered how to breathe again, and it was over.

"My goodness," Maya said after a brief resting spell. "I suppose I *must* love you for sure. My *good*ness!"

"Sure," Forrester said. "And now-if you'll pardon the indelicacy and hand me my pants —" he found he was still puffing a little and paused until he could go on —"I've got an appointment I simply can't afford to miss."

"Oh, all right," Maya said. "But Mr. Forrester —"

He rolled over and looked at her while he began dressing. "I suppose it would be all right if you called me Bill," he said carefully.

"In class, too?"

Forrester shook his head. "No," he said. "Not in class."

"But what I wanted to ask —"

"Yes?" Forrester said.

"Mr. —Bill-do you think I'll pass Introductory World History?"

Forrester considered that question. There was certainly a wide variety of answers he could construct. When he had finished buttoning his shirt he had decided on one.

"I don't see why not," he said, "so long as you complete your assignments regularly."

Nearly two hours later, feeling somewhat light-headed but otherwise in perfectly magnificent fettle, Forrester found himself on the downtown subway. He'd showered and changed and he was whistling a gay little tune as he checked his watch.

The time was five minutes to five. He had just over an hour before he was due to appear at the Tower of Zeus All-Father, but it was better to be a few minutes early than even a single second late.

The train ride was a little bumpy, but Forrester didn't really mind. He was pretty well past being irritated by anything. Nevertheless, he was speculating with just a faint unease as to what the Pontifex Maximus wanted with him. What was in store for him at the strange appointment?

And why all the secrecy?

His brooding was interrupted right away. At 100th Street, a bearded old man got on and sat down next to him. He nudged Forrester in the ribs and muttered: "Look at that now, Daddy-O. Look at that."

"What?" Forrester said, constrained into conversation.

"Damn subways, that's what," the old man said. "Worse every year. Bumpier and slower and worse. Just look around, Daddy-O. Look around."

"I wouldn't quite say —" Forrester began, but the old man gave him another dig in the ribs and cut in:

"Wouldn't say, wouldn't say," he muttered. "Listen, man, there ain't been an improvement in years. You realize that?"

"Well, I —"

"No progress, man, not in more than half a century. Listen, when I was a teen king-War Councilor for the Boppers, I was, and let me tell you that was big time, Daddy-O —when I was a teen king, we were going places. Going places for real. Mars. Venus. We were going to have spaceships, man."

Forrester smiled spasmically at the old man. "I'm sure you —"

"But what happened?" the old man interrupted. "Tell you what happened, man. We never got to Mars and Venus. Mars and Venus came to us instead. Right along with Jupiter and Neptune and Pluto and all the rest of the Gods. And we had no progress ever since that day, Daddy-O, no progress at all and you can believe it."

He dug Forrester in the ribs one final time and sat back with melancholy satisfaction.

"Well," Forrester said mildly, "what good is progress?" The old man, he assured himself after a moment's reflection, wasn't actually saying anything blasphemous. After all, the Gods didn't expect their worshippers to be mindless slaves.

Somehow the notion made him feel happier. He'd have hated reporting the old man. Something in the outdated slang made him feel-almost patriotic. The old man was a part of America, a respected and important part.

The respected part of America made itself felt again in Forrester's ribs. "Progress?" the old man said. "What good's progress? Listen, Daddy-O —how can the human race get anywhere without progress? Answer me that, will you, man? Because it's for-sure real we're not going any place now. No place at all."

"Now look," Forrester said patiently, "progress is an outmoded idea. We've got to be in step with the times. We've got to ask ourselves what progress ever did for us. How did we stand when the Gods returned?" For a brief flash he was back in his history class, but he went on: "Half the world ready to fight the other half with weapons that would have wiped both halves out. You ought to be grateful the Gods returned when they did."

"But we're getting into Nowheresville, man," the old man complained. "We're not in orbit. We can't progress."

Forrester sighed. Why was he talking to the old man, anyway? The answer came to him as soon as he'd asked the question. He wanted to keep his mind off the Tower of Zeus and his own unknown fate there. It was an unpleasant answer; Forrester blanked it out.

"Now, friend," he said. "What have you got? Just what mankind's been looking for all these centuries. Security. You've got security. Nobody's going to blow you to pieces tomorrow. Your job isn't going to vanish overnight. I mean, if you —"

"I got a job," the old man said.

"Really?" Forrester said politely. "What is it?"

"Retired. And it's a tough job, too."

"Oh," Forrester said.

"And anyhow," the old man went on, "what's all this got to do with progress?"

Forrester thought. "Well —"

"Well, nothing," the old man said. "Listen to me, man. I say nothing against the Gods-right? Nothing at all. Wouldn't want to do anything like that. But at the same time, it looks to me like we ought to be able to-reap the fruits of our labors. I read that some place."

"But —"

"In the three thousand years the Gods were gone, we weren't a total loss, man. Not anything like. We discovered a lot. About nature and science and like that. We invented science all by ourselves. So how come the Gods don't let us use it?" The old man dug his elbow once more into Forrester's rib. "How come?"

"The Gods haven't taken anything away from us," Forrester said.

"Haven't they?" the old man demanded. "How about television? Want to answer that one, Daddy-O? Years ago, everybody had a television set. Color and 3-D. The most. The end. Now there's no television at all. Why not? What happened to it?"

"Well," Forrester said reasonably, "what good is television?"

"What good?" Once more Forrester's rib felt the old man's elbow. "Let me tell you —"

"No," Forrester interrupted, suddenly irritated with the whole conversation. "Let *me* tell *you*. The trouble with your generation was that all they wanted to do was sit around on their *glutei maximi* and be entertained. Like a bunch of hypnotized geese. They didn't want to do anything for themselves. Half of them couldn't even read. And now you want to tell me that —"

"Hold it, Daddy-O," the old man said. "You're telling me that the Gods took away television just because we were a bunch of hypnotized geese. That it?"

"That's it."

"Okay," the old man said. "So tell me-what are we now? With the Gods and everything. I mean, man, really-what are we?"

"Now?" Forrester said. "Now you're retired. You're a bunch of retired hypnotized geese."

The doors of the train slid creakily open and Forrester got out onto the 34th Street platform, walking angrily toward a stairway without looking back.

True enough, the old man hadn't committed blasphemy, but it had certainly come close enough there at the end. And if pokes with the elbow weren't declared blasphemous, or at least equivalent to malicious mischief, he thought, there was no justice in the world.

The real trouble was that the man had had no respect for the Gods. There were a good many of the older generation like him. They seemed to feel that humanity had been better off when the Gods had been away. Forrester couldn't see it, and felt vaguely uncomfortable in the presence of someone who believed it. After all, mankind *had* been on the verge of mass suicide, and the Gods had mercifully come back from their self-imposed exile and taken care of things. The exile had been designed to prove, in the drastic laboratory of three thousand years, that Man by himself headed like a lemming for self-destruction. And, for Forrester, the point had been proven.

Yet now that the human race had been saved, there were still men who griped about the Gods and their return. Forrester silently wished the pack of them in Hades, enjoying the company of Pluto and his ilk.

At the corner of 34th and Broadway, as he came out of the subway tunnels, he bought a copy of the *News* and glanced quickly through the headlines. But, as always, there was little sensational news. Mars was doing pretty well for himself, of course: there were two wars going on in Asia, one in Europe and three revolutions in South and Central America. That last did seem to be overdoing things a bit, but not seriously. Forrester shrugged, wondering vaguely when the United States was going to have its turn.

But he couldn't concentrate on the paper and, after a little while, he got rid of it and took a look at his watch.

Twenty to six. Forrester decided he could use a drink to brace himself and steady his nerves. Just one.

On Sixth Avenue, near 34th Street, there was a bar called, for some obscure reason, the *Boat House*. Forrester headed for it, went inside and leaned against the bar. The bartender, a tall man with crew-cut reddish hair, raised his eyebrows in a questioning fashion.

"What'll it be, friend?"

"Vodka and ginger ale," Forrester said. "A double."

It was still, he told himself uneasily, just one drink. And that was all he was going to have.

The bartender brought it and Forrester sipped at it, watching his reflection in the mirror and wishing he felt easier in his mind about the whole Tower of Zeus affair. Then, very suddenly, he noticed that the man next to him was looking at him oddly. Forrester didn't like the look or, for that matter, the man himself, a raw-boned giant with deep-set eyes and a shock of dead-black hair, but so long as nobody bothered him, Forrester wasn't going to start anything.

Unfortunately, somebody bothered him. The tall man leaned over and said loudly: "What's the matter with you, bud? An infidel or something?"

Forrester hesitated. The accusation that he didn't believe in the practices ordained by the Gods themselves was an irritating one. But he could see the other side of the question, too. The tall man was undoubtedly a Dionysian; and, more than that, a member of a small sect inside the general *corpus* of Bacchus/Dionysus worshippers. He held that it was wrong to distill grape or grain products "too far," until there was nothing left but the alcohol.

That meant disapproval of gin and vodka on the grounds that, unlike whiskey or brandy, they'd had the "life" distilled out of them.

Forrester, however, was not really fond of brandy and whiskey. He decided to explain this to the tall man, but at the same time he began to develop the sinking feeling that it wasn't going to do any good.

Oh, well, there was still room for patience. "Don't fire," as Mars had said somewhere, "until you see the whites of their eyes."

"No, I'm no infidel," Forrester said politely. "You see, I'm —"

"No infidel?" the tall man roared. "Then I tell you what you do. You pour that slop out and drink a proper drink." He made a grab for Forrester's glass.

Forrester jerked it back, sloshing it a little in the process-and a few drops splattered on the other's hand.

"Now look here," Forrester said in a reasonable tone of voice. "I —"

"You spilling that stuff on me? What the blazes are you doing that for? I got a good mind to —"

Another man stepped into the altercation. This was a square-built, bullet-headed man with an air that was both truculent and eager. "What's the matter, Herb?" he asked the tall man. "This guy giving you trouble or something?" He favored Forrester with a fierce scowl. Forrester smiled pleasantly back, a little unsure as to how to proceed.

"This guy?" Herb said. *"Trouble?* Sam, he's an *infidel!"*

Forrester said: "I —"

"He drinks vodka," Herb said. "And I guess he drinks gin too."

"Great Bacchus," Sam said in a tone of wonder. "You run into them everywhere these days. Can't get away from the sons of —"

"Now —" Forrester started.

"And not only that," Herb said, "but he spills the stuff on me. Just because I ask him to have a regular drink like a man."

"Spills it on you?" Sam said.

Herb said: "Look," and extended his arm. On the sleeve of his jacket a few spots were slowly drying.

"Well, that's too much," Sam said heavily. "Just too damn much." He scowled at Forrester again. "You know, buddy, somebody ought to teach guys like you a lesson."

Forrester took a swallow of his drink and set the glass down unhurriedly. If either Herb or Sam attacked him, he knew his oath would permit his fighting back. And after the day he'd had, he rather looked forward to the chance. But he had to do his part to hold off an actual fight. "Now look here, friend —"

"Friend?" Sam said. "Don't call me your friend, buddy. I make no friends with infidels."

And, at that point, Forrester realized that he wasn't going to have a fight with Herb or Sam. He was going to have a fight with Herb *and* Sam-and with the third gentleman, a shaggy, beefy man who needed a shave, who stepped up behind them and asked: "Trouble?" in a voice that indicated that trouble was exactly what he was looking for.

"Maybe it is trouble, at that," Herb said tightly, without turning around. "This infidel here's been committing blasphemy."

Three against one wasn't as happy a thought as an even fight had been, but it was too late to back out now. "That's a lie!" Forrester snapped.

"Call me a liar?" Sam roared. He stepped forward and swung a hamlike fist at Forrester's head.

Forrester ducked. The heavy fist swished by his ear harmlessly, and he felt a strange new mixture of elation and fright. He grabbed his vodka-and-ginger from the bar and swung it in a single sweeping arc before him. Liquid rained on the faces of the three men.

Sam was still a little off balance. Forrester slammed the edge of his right hand into his side, and Sam stumbled to the floor. In the same motion, Forrester let fly with the now-empty glass. The shaggy man stood directly in his path. The glass conked him on the forehead and bounced to the floor, where it shattered unnoticed. The shaggy man blinked and Forrester, moving forward, discovered that he had no time to follow matters up in that direction.

Herb was snarling inarticulately, wiping vodka-and-ginger from his eyes. He blocked Forrester's advance toward the shaggy man. Forrester smiled gently and put a hard fist into Herb's solar plexus. The tall man doubled up in completely silent agony.

Forrester took a breath and started forward again. The shaggy man was shaking his head, trying to clear it.

Then Forrester's head became unclear. Something had banged against his right temple and the room was suddenly filled with pain and small, hard stars. Sam, Forrester discovered, had managed to get to his feet. The something had been a small brass ashtray that Sam had thrown at him.

Somehow, he stayed on his feet. The stars were still swirling around him, but he began to be able to see through them, and peered at the figure of the shaggy man, coming at him again. He let his knees bend a little, as if he were going to pass out. The shaggy man seemed to gain confidence from this, and stepped in carefully to kick Forrester in the stomach.

Forrester stepped back, grabbed the upcoming foot, and stood straight, lifting the foot and levering it into the air.

The shaggy man, surprise written all over his shaveless face, went over backward with great abruptness. His head hit the floor with an audible and satisfying *whack*, and then his limbs settled and he remained there, sprawled out and very quiet.

Forrester, meanwhile, was whirling to meet Sam, who was coming in like a bear, his arms outspread and a glaze of hatred in his eyes. Forrester, expressionless, ducked under the man's flailing arms and slammed a fist into his midsection. It was a harder midsection than he'd expected; unlike Herb, Sam had good muscles, and hitting them was like hitting thick rubber. The blow didn't put Sam down. It only made him gasp once.

That was enough. Forrester doubled his right fist and let Sam have one more blow, this one into the face. Sam's mouth opened as his eyes closed. His left arm pawed the air aimlessly for a tenth of a second.

Then he dropped like an empty overcoat.

There was a second of absolute silence. Then Forrester heard a noise behind him and whirled. But it was only Herb, doubled up on the floor and very quietly retching.

Catching his breath, Forrester looked around him. The fight had attracted a lot of attention from the other customers in the bar, but none of them seemed to want to prolong it by joining in.

They were all trying to look as if they were minding their own business, while the bartender...

Forrester stared. The bartender was at the other end of the bar, far away from the scene of action.

He was, as Forrester saw him, just hanging up the telephone.

Forrester put a bill on the bar, turned and walked out into the street. He had absolutely no desire to get mixed up with the secular police.

After all, he had an appointment to keep. And now-after a quiet drink that had turned into a three-against-one battle royal-he had to go and keep it.

CHAPTER 4

It wasn't a very long walk from the *Boat House* to the Tower of Zeus, but it was long enough. By the time Forrester got to the Tower, he was feeling a lot worse than he'd felt when he left the bar. Being perfectly frank with himself, he admitted that he felt terrible.

The blow from the brass ashtray wasn't a sharp pain any longer. It had developed into a nice, dependable ache that had spread all over the side of his head. And his right eye was beginning to swell, probably from the same cause. He'd skinned the knuckles of his right hand, too, probably on Sam's face, and they set up their own smarting.

True, it wasn't a bad list of injuries to result from the odds he'd faced. But that wasn't the point.

You just didn't go up to the Tower of Zeus looking like a back-street brawler.

However, there was no help for it. He straightened his jacket and went in through the Fifth Avenue entrance of the Tower, heading for the first bank of elevators.

Zeus All-Father would know everything about his fight, and would know that it hadn't been his fault. (Hadn't it, though? Forrester asked himself. He remembered the joy he'd felt at the prospect of battle. How far would it count against him?) Zeus All-Father, through his priests, would make what allowances should be made.

Forrester hoped that the Godhead was feeling in a kind and merciful mood.

He reached the bank of elevators, and the burly Myrmidon who stood there, wearing the lightning-bolt shoulder patch of the All-Father. Ahead of him was a chattering crowd of five: mother, father, two daughters and a small son, all obviously out-of-towners. The Tower of Zeus was always a big tourist attraction. The Myrmidon directed them to the stairway that led to the second-floor Arcade, the main attraction for most visitors to the Tower. The Temple of Sacrifice was located up there, while the ground floor was filled with glass-fronted offices of the secretaries of various dignitaries.

Chattering gaily, and looking around them in a kind of happy awe, the family group moved off and Forrester stepped up to the Myrmidon, who said: "Stairway's right over there to your —"

"No," Forrester said. He reached into his jacket pocket, feeling his muscles ache as he did so. He drew out his wallet and managed to extract the simple card he'd been given in the Temple of Pallas Athena, the card which carried nothing but a lightning bolt.

He handed it to the Myrmidon, who looked down at it, frowned, and then looked up.

"What's this for?" he said.

"Well —" Forrester began, and then caught himself. He'd been told not to explain about the card to any mortal. And the Myrmidon was certainly just as mortal as Forrester himself, or any other hireling of the Gods. True, there was always the consideration that he might be Zeus All-Father himself, in disguise.

But that was a consideration that bore no weight at present. Even if the Myrmidon turned out to be a God in disguise, Forrester wouldn't be excused if he said anything about the card. You had to go by appearances; that was the principle on which everything rested, and a very good principle too.

Not that there weren't a few unprincipled young men around who pretended to be Gods in disguise in order to seduce various local and ingenuous maidens. But Zeus always found out about them. And...

Forrester recognized that his thoughts were beginning to veer once more. Without changing his expression, he said evenly: "You're supposed to know," and waited.

The Myrmidon studied him for what seemed about three days. At last he nodded, looked down at the card intently, raised his head and nodded again. "Okay," he said. "Take Car One."

Forrester moved off. Car One was not the first elevator car. As a matter of fact, it was in the middle bank, identified only by a small placard. It took him almost five minutes to find it, and by the time he stepped toward it clocks were ticking urgently in his head.

It would do him absolutely no good to be late.

But another Myrmidon was standing beside the closed doors of the elevator car. Forrester hissed in his breath with impatience-none of which showed on his face-and then caught himself. Certainly Zeus All-Father knew what he was doing, and if Zeus had thrown these delays in his path, it was not for him to complain.

The thought was soothing. Nevertheless, Forrester showed his card to the Myrmidon with an abrupt action very like impatience. This Myrmidon merely glanced at it in a bored fashion and pushed a button on the wall behind him. The elevator doors opened, Forrester stepped inside, and the doors closed.

Forrester was alone in a small bronzed cubicle which began at once to rise rapidly. Just how rapidly, he was unable to tell. There were no indicators at all on the elevator, and the opaque doors made it impossible to see floors flit by. But his ears rang with the speed, and when the car finally stopped, it did so with a slight jerk that threw Forrester, stiff and worried, off balance. He almost fell out of the car as the door opened, and clutched at something for support.

The something was the arm of a Myrmidon. Forrester gaped and looked around. He was in a plain hallway of polished marble. There was no way to tell how many stories above the street he was.

The Myrmidon seemed a more friendly sort than his compatriots downstairs, and wore in addition to the usual lightning-bolt patch the two silver ants of a Captain on the shoulders of his uniform. He nearly smiled at Forrester-but not quite.

"You're William Forrester?" he said.

Forrester nodded. He produced the ID card and handed it with the special card to the Myrmidon.

"Right," the Myrmidon said.

Forrester turned right.

The Myrmidon stared at him. "No," he said. "I mean it's all right. You're all right."

"Thank you," Forrester said.

"Oh —" The Myrmidon looked at him, then shrugged his shoulders. "You're expected," he said at last in a flat voice. "Come with me."

He started down the hallway. Forrester followed him around a corner to an ornate bronzed door, covered with bas-reliefs depicting the actions of the Gods among themselves, and among men. The Myrmidon seemed unimpressed by the magnificence of the thing; he pushed it open and bowed low to, as far as Forrester could see, nobody in particular.

Taking no chances, Forrester copied his bow. He was still bent when the Myrmidon announced: "Forrester is here, Your Concupiscence," in a reverent tone of voice, and backed off a step, narrowly missing Forrester himself in the process.

He waved a hand and Forrester went in.

The door shut halfway behind him.

The room was perfectly unbelievable. Its rich hangings were purple velvet, draping a large window that looked out on...

Forrester gulped. It was impossible to be this high. New York was spread out below like a toy city.

He jerked his eyes away from the window and back to the rest of the room. It was furnished mainly with couches: big couches, little couches, puffy ones, spare ones, in felt, velvet, fur, and every other material Forrester could think of. The rooms were flocked in a pale pink, and on the floor was a deep-purple rug of a richer pile than Forrester had ever seen.

And on one of the couches, the largest and the softest, she reclined.

She was clad only in the diaphanous robes of her calling, and she was stacked. Beside her, little Maya Wilson would have looked about eight years old. Her hair was as red as the inside of a blast furnace, and had about the same effect on Forrester's pulse rate. Her face was a slightly rounded oval, her body a series of mathematically indescribable curves.

Forrester did the only thing he could do.

He bowed again, even lower than before.

"Come in, William Forrester," said the High Priestess of Venus/Aphrodite, the veritable Primate of Venus for New York herself, in a voice that managed to be all at once regal, pleasant and seductive.

Forrester, already in, could think of nothing to say. The gaze of Her Concupiscence fell on the half-open door. "You may retire, Captain," she said to the waiting Myrmidon. "And allow no one to enter here until I give notice."

"Very well, Your Concupiscence," the Myrmidon said.

The door shut.

Forrester snapped erect from his bow, and then realized that he could do nothing but stand there until he had more information. What was the High Priestess of Aphrodite doing in the Tower of Zeus All-Father anyway? And-always supposing she had the right to be there, as of course she must have had-what did she want with William Forrester?

He heaved a great sigh. This was turning into an extremely puzzling day. First there had been the message and the card admitting him to the Tower. Then there had been (the sigh changed in character) Maya Wilson. And then (the sigh changed again, into a faint echo of a groan) the fight in the *Boat House*.

Now he was having an audience with the Primate of Venus for New York.

Why?

The High Priestess's smile gave him no hint. She raised herself to a sitting position and patted the couch. "Sit over here," she said. "Next to me." Then she changed her mind. "No," she added. "First just walk over here, stand up and turn around. Slowly."

Forrester's brain was whirling like a top, but his face was, as usual, expressionless. He did as she had bid him, wondering frantically what was going on, and why?

After he had turned completely around and stood facing her again, the High Priestess simply sat and studied him for almost a full minute, looking him up and down with eyes that were totally unreadable. Forrester waited.

Finally she nodded her head slowly. "You'll do," she said, in a reflective tone, and nodded her head again. "Yes, you'll do."

Forrester couldn't restrain his questions any longer. "*Do?*" he burst out. "I mean," he continued, more quietly, "what will I do for, Your Concupiscence?"

"Oh, for whatever honor it is that our beloved Goddess has in mind for you," the High Priestess said offhandedly. "I can certainly see that you will do. A little pudgy around the middle, but that's a trifle and hardly matters. The important things are there. You're obviously strong and quick."

At that point Forrester caught up with the first sentence of her explanation. "The-the Goddess?" he said faintly.

"Certainly," the High Priestess said. "Else why would I give you audience? I am not promiscuous in my dealings with the lay world."

"I'm sure," Forrester said respectfully.

The High Priestess looked at him sardonically. "Of course you are," she said. "However, the important thing is that our beloved Aphrodite has selected you, William Forrester, for some high honor."

Forrester caught her word for the Goddess, and remembered, thanking his lucky stars he hadn't had a chance to slip, that here in the Tower it was protocol to refer to the Gods and Goddesses by their Greek names alone.

"I don't suppose," he said tentatively, "that you have any idea just what this-high honor is?"

"You, William Forrester," the High Priestess began, in some rage, "dare to question —" Her tone changed. "Oh, well, I suppose I shouldn't become angry with ...No." She shrugged, but her tone carried a little pique. "Frankly, I don't know what the honor is."

"Well, then," Forrester said, his bearing perfectly calm, even though he could feel his stomach sinking to ground level, "how do you know it's an honor?" The thought that had crossed his mind was almost too horrible to retain, but he had to say it. "Perhaps," he went on, "I've offended the Gods in some unusual way-some way very offensive to them."

"Perhaps you have."

"And perhaps," Forrester said, "they've decided on some exquisite method of punishing me. Something like the punishment they gave Tantalus when he —"

"I know the ways of the Gods quite well, thank you," the High Priestess said coolly. "And I can tell you that your fears have no justification."

"But —"

"Please," the High Priestess said, raising a hand. "If the Gods were to punish you, they would simply have sent out a squad of Myrmidons to pick you up, and that would have been the end of it."

"Perhaps not," Forrester said, in a voice that didn't sound at all like his own to him. It sounded much too unconcerned. "Perhaps I have offended only the Goddess herself." The idea sounded more plausible the more he thought about it. "Certainly the All-Father would back up his favorite Daughter in punishing a mortal."

"Certainly he would. There is no doubt of that. And still the Myrmidons would have —"

"Not necessarily. You're well aware of the occasional arguments and quarrels between the Gods."

"I am," the High Priestess said, not without irony. "And it does not appear seemly that an ordinary mortal should mention —"

"I teach History," Forrester said. "I know of such quarrels. Especially between Athena and Aphrodite."

"And?"

"It's obvious. Since I'm an acolyte of Athena, it may be that Aphrodite wished to keep my arrest secret."

"I doubt it," the High Priestess said.

Forrester wished he could believe her. But his own theory looked uncomfortably plausible. "It certainly looks as if I'm right."

"Well —" For a second the High Priestess paled visibly, the freckles that went with her red hair standing out clearly on her face and giving her the disturbing appearance of an eleven-year-old. No eleven-year-old, however, Forrester reminded himself, had ever been built like the High Priestess.

Then she regained her color and laughed, all in an instant. "For a minute," she said in a light tone, "you almost convinced me of your forebodings. But there's nothing in them. There couldn't be."

Forrester opened his mouth, and *Why not?* was on his lips. But he never got a chance to say the words. The High Priestess blinked and peered more closely at his face, and before he had a chance to speak she asked him: "What happened to you?"

"A small accident," Forrester said quickly. It was a lie, but he thought a pardonable one. The truth was just too complicated to spin out; he had no real intent to deceive.

But the High Priestess shook her head. "No," she said. "Not an accident. A fight. Your hands are skinned and bruised."

"Very well," Forrester said. "It was a fight. But I was attacked, and entitled to defend myself."

"I'm sure," the High Priestess said. "Yet I have a question for you. Who won?"

"Won? I did. Naturally."

It sounded boastful, he reflected, but it wasn't. He had won, and it had been natural to him to do so. His build and strength, as well as his speed, had made any other outcome unlikely.

And the High Priestess didn't seem to take offense. She said only: "I thought so. Just a moment." Then she walked over to a telephone. It was a simple act but Forrester watched it fervently. First she stood up, and then she took a step, and then another step ...and her whole body moved. And moved.

It was marvelous. He watched her bend down to pick up the phone without any clear idea of the meaning of the motions. The motions themselves were enough. Every curve and jiggle and bounce was engraved forever on his mind.

The High Priestess dialed a number, waited and said: "Aphrodite's compliments to Hermes the Healer."

An indistinguishable voice answered her from the receiver.

"Aphrodite thanks you," the High Priestess said, "and asks if Hermes might send one of his priests around for a few minor ministrations."

The receiver said something else.

"No," the High Priestess said. "Nothing like that. Don't you think we have other interests-such as they are?"

Again the receiver.

"Just a black eye and some skin lacerations," the High Priestess said. "Nothing serious."

And the receiver replied once more.

"Very well," the High Priestess said. "Aphrodite wishes you well." She hung up.

She came back to the couch, Forrester's eyes following her every inch of the way. She sat down, looked up and said: "What's the matter? Do I bore you?"

"*Bore* me?" Forrester all but cried.

"It's just-well, nothing, I suppose," the High Priestess said. "Your expression."

"Training," Forrester explained. "An acolyte does well not to express his emotions too clearly."

The High Priestess nodded casually and patted the couch at her side. "Sit down here, next to me."

Forrester did so, gingerly.

A moment of silence ensued.

Then Forrester, gathering courage, said: "Thank you for getting a Healer. But I'd like to ask you —"

"Yes?"

"How do you know I'm not under some sort of carefully concealed arrest? After all, you said before that you were sure —"

"And I am sure," the High Priestess said. "Aphrodite herself has ordered a sacrifice in her favor. A sacrifice from you. And Aphrodite does not accept-much less *order* —a sacrifice from those standing in her disfavor."

"You're —"

"I'm sure," the High Priestess said.

"Oh," Forrester said. "Good." The world was not quite as black as it could have been. And still, it was not exactly shining white. A sacrifice? And outside the door, Forrester could hear a disturbance.

What did that mean?

Her Concupiscence didn't seem to hear it at first. "We will perform the rite together and —" The noise grew louder. "What's that?" she said.

It was the sound of argument. Forrester realized what had happened. "It's the priest from Hermes," he said. "The Healer. You forgot to tell the Captain of Myrmidons to let him in."

"My goodness!" the High Priestess said. "So I did! It slipped my mind entirely." She touched Forrester's cheek affectionately. "Of course, I imagine it's only natural to be a bit forgetful when —" She got up and went to the door.

The Captain and a small, fat priest in a golden-edged tunic were tangled confusedly outside. The High Priestess looked away from them in disdain and said regally: "You may permit the Healer to enter, Captain." The tangle came untied and the little priest scooted in. To him, as the door closed again, the High Priestess whispered: "Sorry. I didn't expect you quite so soon."

"No more did I!" The priest waved his caduceus furiously, so that it seemed as if the twin snakes twined round it were moving, the two wings above them beating, and the ball surmounting all, on top of the staff, traced uneasy designs in the air. "Myrmidons!" he said.

"I certainly regret —"

"If you boiled down their brains for the fat content, one alone would supply the Temple with candles for a year! Just beef and nothing more! Beef! Beef!"

Then, with a start, he seemed to see the High Priestess for the first time, and his tone changed. "Oh," he said. "Good evening, Your Concupiscence."

"Good evening," the High Priestess said in an indulgent tone.

"Well, well, well," the priest said. "What seems to be the trouble? My goodness. It must be important, sure enough-certainly important." His little round red eager face seemed to shine as he went on. "Hermes himself transported me here just as soon as you called!"

"Really?"

"Oh, my, yes," the priest said. "Just as soon as ever. Yes. Hm. And you can believe me when I tell you-believe me, Your Concupiscence-take my word when I tell you —"

"Yes?"

"Hermes," the priest said. "Hermes doesn't often take such an interest —I may say such a *personal* interest-in a mortal, I'll tell you. And you can believe me when I do tell you that. I do."

"I'm sure," the High Priestess said.

"Yes," the priest said, waving his caduceus gently. He blinked. "Where's the patient? The mortal?"

"He's over here," the High Priestess said, motioning to Forrester sitting awestruck on the couch. Priests of Hermes were common enough sights-but a priest like this was something new and strange in his experience.

"Ah," the priest said, twinkling at him. "So there you are, eh? Over there? You *are* sitting over *there*, aren't you?"

"That's right," Forrester said blankly.

"Now listen to me carefully," the High Priestess said. "You're not to ask his name, or mention anything about this visit to anyone-understand?"

The priest blinked. "Oh, certainly. Absolutely. Without doubt. I've already been told that, you might say. Already. Certainly. Wouldn't think of such a thing." He moved over and stood near Forrester, peering down at him. "My goodness," he said. "Let me see that eye, young man."

Forrester turned his head wordlessly.

"Oh, my, yes," the priest said. "Black indeed. Very black. A fight. My, yes. An altercation, disagreement, discussion, battle —"

"Yes," Forrester cut in.

"Certainly you have," the priest said. "And what'd the other fellow look like, eh? Beaten, I'll bet. You look a strong type."

Forrester relaxed. It was the only thing to do while the priest babbled on, touching his wounds gently as he did so with various parts of his caduceus. The pain vanished with a touch of the left wingtip, and the lacerations healed instantly as they were caressed with first one and then another of the various coils of the snakes.

But Forrester now was free to worry. Arrest was out of the question. As the High Priestess had said, on the evidence it was clear that Aphrodite intended to honor him in some way. And there was nothing at all, he thought, wrong with an honor from the Goddess of Love.

But another sacrifice? After the sacrifice to Aphrodite he'd made earlier, and the fight he'd gotten into, he just didn't quite feel up to it. It wouldn't do to refuse, but...

"Well," the priest said, stepping back. "Well, well. You ought to be all right now, young fellow-right as rain."

Forrester said: "Thanks."

"Might feel a little soreness-tenderness, you might say-for a day or so. Only a day or so, tenderness," the priest said. "After that, right as rain. Right as you'll ever be. *All* right, as a matter of fact: all right."

Forrester said: "Thanks."

The priest went to the door, turned, and said to the High Priestess: "Hermes' blessing on you both, as a matter of fact, as they say. Blessings from Hermes on you both."

The High Priestess nodded regally.

"And," the priest said, "merely by the way, as it might be, without meaning harm, if you would ask a blessing for me-Aphrodite's blessing? Easy for you. Of course, it would be nice curing-curing, as they say-stupidity, plain dumbness, as they call such things-curing stupidity as easily as I can cure small ills. Nice."

"Indeed," the High Priestess said.

"But there," the priest went on. "Only the Gods can cure that. Only the Gods and no one else. Yes. Hm. And not often. They don't do anything like that in the-ah-regular course of things. As a matter of fact, you might say, I've never heard of-never heard of such a case. Never. Not one. Yet ..." He opened the door, spat: "Myrmidons!" and disappeared into the hallway.

The door banged shut.

Forrester sighed heavily. The High Priestess turned to him.

"Feel better?" she asked.

"Much," Forrester said, dreading the ordeal to come.

The High Priestess came over to the couch and sat down next to him. She put a hand on his shoulder. "Shall we prepare for the-sacrifice?"

Forrester sighed again. "Sure," he said. "Naturally."

When she was locked in his arms, it was as if time had started all over again. Forrester responded to the eagerness of the woman as he'd never dreamed he could respond; all his tiredness dropped away as if it had never been, and he was a new man. He touched her bare flesh and felt the heat of her through his fingers and hands; with his arms around her nakedness he rolled, locked to her, feeling the friction of skin against skin and the magnificence of her.

The sacrifice went on ...and on ...and on into endless time and endless space. Forrester thrust and gasped at the woman and her head went back, her mouth pulled open as she shivered and responded to him....

Forever....

Until finally they lay, panting, in the magnificent room. Forrester rose first, vaguely surprised at himself. He found a towel in a closet at the far end of the room and wiped his damp forehead slowly.

"Well," he said. "That was quite a sacrifice. What next?"

The High Priestess raised herself on one elbow and stared across the room at him. "There is no need for such familiarity, Forrester," she said. "Not from a lay acolyte."

Forrester tossed the towel onto a couch. "My apologies, Your Concupiscence. I'm a little-light-headed. But what happens next?"

The High Priestess reached into the diaphanous pile of her clothing and came up with a small diamond-encrusted watch she wore, usually, on her wrist. "Our timing was almost perfect," she said. "It is now twenty-hundred hours. The Goddess expects you at twenty-oh-one exactly."

A hurried half-minute passed. Then, fully dressed, Forrester went with the High Priestess to a golden door half-hidden in the hangings at the side of the room. She made a series of mystical signs: the circle, the serpent and others Forrester couldn't quite follow.

She opened the door, genuflecting as she did so, and Forrester dropped to one knee behind her, looking at the doorway.

It was filled with a pale blue haze that looked like the clear summer sky on a hot day. Except that it wasn't sky, but a curtain that wavered and shimmered before his eyes. Beyond it, he could see nothing.

The High Priestess rose from her genuflection and Forrester followed suit. There was a sole second of silence.

Then the High Priestess said: "You are to step through the Veil of Heaven, William Forrester."

Forrester said: "*Me?* Through the *Veil of Heaven?*"

"Don't be afraid," she said. "And don't try to touch the Veil. Just walk through as if nothing at all were there."

Forrester filled his lungs as though he were going to take a very high dive. He thought: *Here goes nothing*. That was all; there wasn't time for anything else.

He stepped into the blue haze, and had a sudden sensation of falling.

"And what I offer you is a chance to rule this world with me-at a price, of course!"

CHAPTER 5

There was a tingle like a mild electric shock. Forrester opened his mouth and then closed it again as the tingle stopped, and the sense of falling simply died away. He had closed his eyes on the way into the curtain, and now he opened them again.

He closed them very quickly, counted to ten, and took a deep breath. Then he opened them to look at the room he was in.

It was unlike any room he had ever seen before. It didn't have the opulence of the High Priestess's rooms. I am a room, it seemed to say, and a room is what I was meant to be. I don't have to draw attention to myself like my poorer sisters. I am content merely to exist as the room of rooms, the very type and image of the Ideal Enclosure.

The floors and walk of the place seemed to blend into each other at odd angles. Forrester's eyes couldn't quite follow them or understand them, and judging the size of the room was out of the question. There was a golden wash of light filling the room, though it didn't seem to come from anywhere in particular. It was, in fact, as if the room itself were shining. Forrester blinked and rubbed his eyes. The light, or whatever it was, was changing color.

Gradually, he realized that it went on doing that. He wasn't sure that he liked it, but it was certainly different. The colors went from gold to pale rose to violet to blue, and so on, back to gold again, while little eddies and swirls of light sparkled into rainbows here and there.

Forrester began to feel dizzy again.

There were various objects standing around here and there in the room, but Forrester couldn't quite tell what they were. Even their sizes were difficult to judge, because of the shifting light and shape of the room itself. There was only one thing that seemed reasonably certain.

He was alone in the room.

Set in one wall was a square of light that didn't change color quite as much as everything else. Forrester judged it to be a window and headed for it. With his first step, he discovered something else about the place.

The carpeting was completely unique. Instead of fiber, the floor seemed to have been covered a foot deep with foam rubber. Forrester didn't exactly walk to the window; he bounced there. The sensation was almost enjoyable, he thought, when you got used to it. He wondered just how long it took to get used to it and settled on eighty years as a good first guess.

He stood in front of the window. He looked out.

He saw nothing but clouds and sky.

It took a long while for him to decide what to do next, and when he finally did come to a decision, it was the wrong one.

He looked down.

Below him there were tumbled rocks, ledges of ice and snow, clouds and-far, far below-the flat land of the Earth. He wanted to shut his eyes, but he couldn't. The whole vast stomach-churning panorama spread out beneath him endlessly. The people below, if there were any, weren't even big enough to be ants. They were completely invisible. Forrester took a deep breath and gripped the side ledges of the window.

And a voice behind him said: "Welcome, Mortal."

Forrester almost went through the window. But he managed to regain his balance and turn around, saying angrily: "Don't *do* that!" As the last of the words left his lips, he became aware of the smiling figure facing him.

She was standing in a spotlight, Forrester thought at first. Then he saw that the light was coming from the woman herself-or from her clothing. The dress she wore was a satinlike sheath that glowed with an aura even brighter than the room. Her blonde hair picked up the radiance and glowed, too, illuminating a face that was at once regal, inviting and passionate. It was, Forrester thought, a hell of a disturbing combination.

The cloth of the dress clung to her figure as if it wanted to. Forrester didn't blame it a bit; the dress showed off a figure that was not only beyond his wildest dreams, but a long way beyond what he had hitherto regarded as the bounds of possibility. From shoulder to toe, she was perfection.

This was also true of the woman from shoulder to crown.

Forrester gulped and, automatically, went on one knee.

"Please," he murmured. "Pardon me. I didn't mean —"

"Quite all right," the Goddess murmured. "I understand perfectly."

"But I —"

"Never mind all that now," Venus said, with just a hint of impatience. "Rise, William Forrester-or you who were William Forrester."

Forrester rose. Sweat was pouring down his face. He made no effort to wipe it away. "Were?" he asked, dazed. "But that's my name!"

"It *was,*" Venus said, in the same calm tone. "Henceforth, your name is Dionysus."

Forrester took a while to remember to swallow. "Dionysus?" he said at last.

There was another silence.

Forrester, feeling that perhaps his first question could use some amplification, said: "Dionysus? Bacchus? You mean me?"

"Quite right," Venus said. "That will be your name, and you'd better begin getting used to it."

"Now wait a minute!" he said. "I don't mean to be disrespectful, but something occurs to me. I mean, it's the first thing I thought of, and I'm probably wrong, but just let me ask the questions, if you don't mind, and maybe some of this will make some sense. Because just a few hours ago I was doing very nicely on my own and I —"

"What are your questions?" Venus said.

Forrester swayed. "Dionysus/Bacchus himself," he said. "Won't he mind my —"

Venus laughed. "Mind your using his name? My goodness, no."

"But —"

"It's all because of the orgies," Venus said.

Everything, he told himself, was getting just a little too much for him. "Orgies?" he said.

Venus nodded. "You see, there are all those orgies held in his honor. You know about those, of course."

"Sure I do," Forrester said, watching everything narrowly. In just a few seconds, he told himself hopefully, the whole room would vanish and he would be in a nice, peaceful insane asylum.

"Well, it isn't impossible for a God to be at all the orgies held in his honor," Venus said. "Naturally not. But, at the same time, they are all rather boring-for a God, I mean. And that's why you're here," she finished.

Forrester said: "Oh." And then he said: "Oh?" The room hadn't disappeared yet, but he was willing to give it time.

"Dionysus," Venus said patiently, as if she were explaining the matter to a small and rather ugly child, "gets tired of appearing at the orgies. He wants someone to take his place."

The silence after that sentence was a very long one. Forrester could think of nothing to say but: *"Me?"*

"You will be raised to the status of Godling," Venus said. "You remember Hercules and Achilles, don't you?"

"Never met them," Forrester said vacantly.

"Naturally," Venus said. "They were, however, ancient heroes, raised to the status of Godling, just as you yourself will be. However, you will not be honored or worshipped under your own name."

Forrester nodded. "Naturally," he said, wondering what he was talking about. There was, he realized, the possibility that he was not insane after all, but he didn't want to think about that. It was much too painful.

"You will receive instructions in the use of certain powers," Venus said. "These will enable you to perform your new duties."

Duties.

The word carried a strange connotation. Dionysus/Bacchus was the God of wine, among other things, and women and song had been thrown in as an afterthought. The duties of a stand-in for a God like that sounded just a little bit overwhelming.

"These-duties," he said. "Will they be temporary or permanent?"

"Well," Venus said, "that depends." She smiled at him sweetly.

"Depends?"

"So far," Venus said, "our testing shows that you are capable of handling certain of the duties to be entrusted to you. But, for the rest, everything depends on your own talents and devotion."

"Ah," Forrester said, and then: "Testing?"

"You don't suppose that we would pick a mortal for an important job like this without making certain that he was capable of doing the job, do you?"

"Frankly," Forrester said, "I haven't got around to supposing anything yet."

Venus smiled again. "We have tested you," she said, "and so far you appear perfectly capable of exercising your powers."

Forrester blinked. "Exercising?"

"Exactly. As a street brawler, for instance, you do exceptionally well."

"As a —"

"How does your face feel?" she asked.

"My what?" Forrester said. "Oh. Face. Fine. Street brawls, you said?"

"I did," Venus said. "My goodness, the way you bashed that one bruiser with your drink-that was really excellent. As a matter of fact, I feel it incumbent on me to tell you that I haven't enjoyed a fight so much in years."

Wondering whether he should be complimented or just a little ashamed of himself, Forrester said nothing at all. The idea that he had been under the personal supervision of Aphrodite herself bothered him more than he could say. The brawl was the first thing that came to mind. It didn't seem like the sort of thing a Goddess of Love ought to have been watching.

And then he thought of the High Priestess.

He felt a blush creeping up around his collar, and was thankful only that it was not visible under the tan of his skin. He remembered who had ordered the sacrificial rites, and thought bitterly and guiltily about spectator sports.

But his face remained perfectly calm.

"So far," Venus said, "I must say that you have come through with flying colors. You should be proud of yourself."

Forrester didn't feel exactly proud. He wanted to crawl into a hole and die there.

"Well," he said, "I —"

"But there is more," Aphrodite said.

"More?"

The idea didn't sound attractive. In spite of what one of the tests had involved, the notion of any more tests was just a little fatiguing. Besides, Forrester was not at all sure that he would be at his best, when he knew that dispassionate observers were chronicling his technique and his every movement.

How much more, he wondered, could he take?

And, he reflected, how much more of *what*?

"We must be certain," Aphrodite said, "that you can prove yourself worthy of the dignity of a Godling."

"Ah," Forrester said cleverly. "So there are going to be more tests?"

"There are," Venus said. "After all, you will be expected to act as the *alter persona* of Dionysus. That involves responsibilities almost beyond the ken of a mortal."

Wine, Forrester thought wildly, women and song.

He wondered if he were going to be asked to sing something. He couldn't remember anything except the *Star Spangled Banner* and an exceptionally silly rhyme from his childhood. Neither of them seemed just right for the occasion.

"You must learn to behave as a true God," Venus said. "And we must know whether you are fitted for the part."

Forrester nodded. The one thing keeping him sane, he reflected, was the hope of insanity. But the room was still there, and Venus was standing near him, talking quietly away.

"Thus," she said, "there must be further tests, so that we may be sure of your capacities."

Capacities? Just what was *that* supposed to mean? "I see," he lied. "And suppose I fail?"

"Fail?"

"Suppose I don't live up to expectations," Forrester said.

"Well, then," Venus declared, "I'm afraid the Gods might be angry with you."

Forrester had no doubt whatever as to the meaning of the words. Either he lived up to expectations or he didn't live at all. The Gods' anger was not a small affair, and it seldom satisfied itself with small results. When a God got angry with you, you simply hoped the result would be quick. You didn't really dare hope it would also be temporary.

Forrester passed a hand over his forehead. If he had been doing his own picking, he thought a little sadly, the job of tryout stand-in for Dionysus was not the job he would have chosen. But then, the choice wasn't his, and it never had been. It was the Gods who had picked him.

Unfortunately, if he failed, the mistake wouldn't be laid at the door of the Gods. It would be laid at the door of William Forrester, together with a nice, big, black funeral wreath.

But it didn't sound too bad at that, he told himself hopefully. After all, it wasn't every day that a man was offered the job of stand-in for a God, not every day that a man was offered the chance of passing a lot of strenuous and embarrassing tests, and dying if he failed.

He told himself sternly to look on the positive side, but all he could think of was the succession of tests still to come. What would they be like? How could he ever pass them all? What would be thought necessary to establish a man as a first-rate double for Dionysus?

Looks, he thought, were obviously the first thing, and he certainly had those. For a second he almost wished he could see Ed Symes and apologize for getting mad when Ed had told him he looked like Bacchus.

But then, he reflected, he didn't want to go too far. The idea of apologizing to Ed Symes, no matter who his sister was, made Forrester's gorge rise about five and a half feet.

"However," Aphrodite went on, as if she had just thought of something too unimportant to bother mentioning, "don't worry about it. My father's thunderbolt needn't concern you. I have every confidence that you will prove yourself."

She smiled radiantly at him.

The idea occurred to Forrester that she just didn't think that a mortal's mortality was important. But the idea didn't stay long. Being reassured by a Goddess, he told himself confusedly, was very reassuring.

Venus was looking him up and down speculatively, and Forrester suddenly thought a new test was coming. A little gentle sweat began to break out on his forehead again, but his face stayed calm. He took a deep breath and tried to concentrate on gathering strength. The High Priestess had been something special but, Forrester thought, she had not really called out his *all*. Venus was clearly another matter.

But Venus said only: "Those clothes," in a considering sort of tone.

"Clothes?" Forrester said, trying to readjust in a hurry.

"You certainly can't go in those clothes. Hera would object quite violently, I'm afraid. She's awfully stuffy about such things."

The intimate details about the Gods intrigued Forrester. "Stuffy? Hera?"

"Confidentially," Venus said, "at times, the All-Mother can be an absolute bitch."

She went over to one of the light-swirled walls, and a part of the light seemed to fade as she did so. Of course, she did nothing so crude as opening a door. When she started for the wall there was no closet apparent there, but when she arrived it was there, solid, and open.

It was just that simple.

She took out a white robe and started back. Forrester took his eyes from her with an effort and watched the closet disappear again. By the time she had reached him, it was only a part of the swirling wall again.

And the hospital attendants were nowhere in sight.

She handed Forrester the robe. He took it warily, but it seemed real enough. At any rate, it was as real as anything else that was happening to him, he thought.

It was a simple tunic, cut in the style of the ancient Greek *chiton*, and open at one side instead of the front. Forrester turned it in his hands. At the waist and shoulder there was a golden clasp to hold it in place. The clasp wasn't figured in any special way. The material itself was odd: it was an almost fluorescent white and, though it was perfectly opaque, it was thinner than any paper Forrester had ever seen in public. It almost didn't seem to be there when he rubbed it between his thumb and forefinger.

"Well, don't just stand there," Venus said. "Get started."

"Started?" Forrester said.

"Get dressed. The others are waiting for you."

"Others?"

But she didn't answer. Forrester looked frantically around the room for anything that looked even remotely like a dressing room. As a last resort, he was willing to settle for a screen. No room, no screen. He was willing to settle for a chair he could crouch behind. There was none.

He looked hopefully at the Goddess. Perhaps, he thought, she would leave while he dressed. She showed no sign of doing so. He cleared his throat and jerked at his collar nervously.

"Now, now," Venus said sternly. "Don't tell me the presence of your Goddess embarrasses you." She raised her head imperiously. "Hurry it up."

Very slowly, he began taking off his clothes. There was, after all, nothing to be ashamed of, he told himself. As a matter of fact, Venus ought to be getting used to the sight of him undressing by this time.

Somehow, he finally managed to get the *chiton* on straight. Venus looked him over and nodded her approval.

"Come along now," she said. "They're waiting for us. And one thing: don't get nervous, for Hera's sake. You're all right."

"Oh," Forrester said. "Sure. Perfectly all right. Right as rain."

"Well, you are. As a matter of fact, I think you'll make a fine Dionysus."

She led him toward a wall opposite where the closet had been. As they approached it, a section of it became bluer and bluer. With a sinking feeling, Forrester told himself that he knew what was coming.

He did. The wall dissolved into the shimmering blue haze of a Veil of Heaven, just like the one that had transported him from New York to his present position. Where that was, he wasn't entirely sure, but remembering his one look out the window, he suspected it was Mount Olympus.

But there wasn't any time for thinking. Venus took his hand coolly as they reached the blue haze. Then both of them stepped through.

CHAPTER 6

The room into which they stepped seemed even larger than the one they had left. The distances were just as hard to measure, and why Forrester had the feeling, he couldn't have said, but it did feel larger. The sense of enormous space hung over it.

The wall colors were just the same, however, dripping and changing in a continuous flow of patterns, with the little sunbursts and rainbows appearing here and there without any visible reason.

But the room itself was comparatively unimportant, Forrester knew. It was what went on in the room that sent shivers up his spine, and instructed one knee to start knocking against other one. He had heard of the Court of the Gods, though as far as he knew no mortal had ever seen it. There were certainly no photographs of it, even in the most exhaustive travel books.

Forrester knew without question that he was standing in that Courtroom. The knowledge did not make him calm. And the beings sitting and reclining on couches along the shimmering walls made him feel even worse. He recognized every one of them, and every one sent a new shock of awe running through his nerves. His stomach felt like a hard rubber handball.

There was Zeus All-Father, with his great, silvery, ringleted beard. His hands were combing through it and he was frowning majestically into the distance. Next to him was the imperious Hera, Mother of the Gods. She sat with her hands folded in her lap, as if she were waiting for the end of the world to be announced. There was Mars, tough and hairy-chested, scratching his side with one hand and scowling horribly. His fierce, bearded face looked somehow out of place without the battle helmet that usually topped it. The horned and goat-legged Pan was there, and Vulcan, crippled and ugly with his squat body and giant arms, reclining like an ape on a couch all alone, and motherly looking Ceres using one hand to pat her hair as if she, not Forrester, were the nervous one.

Athena was there, too, lovely and gray-eyed. She seemed to be smiling at him with special favor, and Forrester felt grateful.

He needed all the help he could get.

But the other Gods were absent. Where were they? Pluto and Phoebus Apollo were missing, and so were Mercury, Neptune, Dionysus and Diana.

And...

"Ah," the great voice of Zeus boomed, as Forrester and Venus stepped through the Veil. Forrester heard the voice and shuddered. "The mortal is here," Zeus went on in his awe-inspiring roar. "Welcome, Mortal!"

Forrester opened his mouth, but Hera got in ahead of him.

She leaned over to her divine husband and hissed, in a tone audible to everyone in the room: "Don't belabor the obvious, dear. Enough's enough."

"It is?" Zeus said. The roar was exactly the same. "I'm not at all sure. No! Of course not. Naturally not, my dear. Naturally not." He looked around slowly, nodding his great head. "Now, now. Let's see. Do we have a quorum? I don't see Morpheus. Where's Morpheus?"

"Asleep, as usual," Mars growled. He finished scratching his side and began on his beard. "Where else would the old fool be? He's nothing but a bore anyway and I say to Hades with him. Let's get on."

"Now, Ares," Pallas Athena said mildly. "Don't be crude."

"Crude?" Mars bellowed. "All I said was that the old bore's not here. It's true, isn't it? What in Hades is so crude about it?"

"Hah!" Vulcan growled, in a bass voice that seemed to come from the bottom of a large barrel. "Look who mentions being a bore."

"Why, you —" Mars started.

"Children!" Hera snapped at once.

There was quiet, and Forrester had time to get dizzy. Maybe, he thought, he had been traveling too much. After all, he had started in New York, and then he had found himself on what he suspected was Mount Olympus, in Greece. And now he was somewhere else.

He wasn't entirely sure where. The Court of the Gods existed; he knew that. But he had never heard just where it existed, and it was entirely possible that no mortal knew. In which case, Forrester thought confusedly, I don't even know where I am.

For the first time, he began to think seriously that, perhaps, he was sane after all. Maybe everything he was seeing and hearing was true. It was certainly beginning to look that way. And, in that case, maybe the dizziness he felt was just airsickness, or spacesickness, or whatever kind of sickness came from traveling through those blue Veils.

At least, he told himself, thinking of the old man he had met on the way downtown, at least it beat the subway.

He looked behind him. He and Venus were standing in the center of the room. There was no blue veil behind them. It had, apparently, done its duty and gone away.

The subway, Forrester told himself solemnly, didn't do that.

Zeus cleared his throat ponderously. "I count eight of us," he said. "Eight, all told. Of course, that's eight without the mortal." He paused, and then added: "If you count the mortal in, there are nine."

Pan stirred. "That's a quorum," he announced in a hoarse voice that had a heavy vibrato in it. It reminded Forrester, oddly, of the bleating of a goat. Pan crossed his legs and his hooves clashed, striking sparks. "Pluto and Poseidon said they'd accept our judgment."

"Why the absence?" Vulcan said shortly.

"A storm, I think," Pan said. "Out in the North Atlantic, if memory serves-and it does. As far as I recall, there are four ships sunk so far. Quite an affair."

Vulcan said: "Ah," and reclined again.

Hera leaned forward. "Where's Apollo? He said he might come."

"Sure he did," Mars said heavily. "Old Sunshine Boy never misses a bit of excitement. Only he probably found something even more exciting. He's in California, all dressed up as a mortal."

"California?" Ceres said. "My goodness, what would that boy be doing in California?"

Mars guffawed. "Probably showing off-how Sunshine Boy loves to show off! Displaying that gorgeous body to the girls on Muscle Beach, I'll bet."

"Eight to five," Pan said at once.

Mars turned to him and nodded shortly. "Done."

"Now, if I were a betting man," Vulcan began in a thoughtful bass, "I'd —"

"We all know what you'd do, Gimpy," Mars roared. "But you won't do it, so shut up about it."

"Please," Hera said. "Order." Her voice was like chilled steel. The others settled back. "I think we're ready. Shall we begin, dear?" She looked at Zeus, who got ready to start. But before he could get a word out, there was a flicker of blue energy in the room, a couple of yards away from Forrester and Venus. The flicker expanded to a Veil, and a man stepped out of it.

He was a short, fat individual wearing a *chiton* as if he had slept in it for three or four weeks. His face was puffy and his golden hair was ruffled. His eyelids seemed to have acquired a permanent half-mast, and beneath them the eyes were bleary and disinterested.

Forrester needed no introductions to Morpheus, the God of Sleep.

The God looked around at the assembled company with a kindly little smile on his tired face. Then, slowly and luxuriously, he yawned. When his mouth closed again, after a view of caverns measureless to man, he rubbed at his eyes with his knuckles, and then heaved a great sigh and, apparently, resigned himself to the terrible effort of speech.

"I'm late," he said. "But it's really not my fault."

"Oh?" Hera said in a nasty tone of voice.

Morpheus shook his head slowly from side to side. "It really isn't." His voice was terribly calm. It was obvious, Forrester thought, that he did not give a damn. "The alarm just didn't seem to go off again. Or else I didn't hear it."

"Now, Morpheus," Hera said. "I should think you'd get some kind of alarm that really worked, after all this time."

"Why bother?" Morpheus said, and shrugged ponderously. "Anyhow, I'm here." He yawned again. "The thing's tiresome, but I did say I'd be here, and here I am. Now, does that satisfy everybody? Because if it doesn't, I do have some sleep to catch up on."

"It satisfies us all," Hera said with some asperity. "Go sit down."

Morpheus shambled quietly over to a couch near Mars. He lowered himself onto it, and slowly slipped from a sitting position to a reclining one.

"Well," Hera said to Zeus, "we're ready, dear."

"Oh," Zeus said. "Oh. Certainly. I declare this meeting—I declare this meeting fully met." He cleared his throat with a rumble that shook the air. "We're here, as I suppose you all know, to consider the problem of William Forrester. But first, I am reminded of a little story I picked up on Earth, and in the hopes that some of you here might not have heard it, I—"

"We've heard it," Hera said, "and, anyhow, this is neither the time nor the place."

Zeus turned to look at her. He shrugged. "Very well," he said equably. "Let us return to William Forrester, as a possible substitute for Dionysus. The first consideration ought to be the psychological records, wouldn't you say?"

"I would," Hera said through her teeth.

"I believe Athena is in charge of that department, and if she is ready to report—"

"Of course she's ready," Hera said, "dear."

Zeus nodded. "Well, then, what are we waiting for?"

Athena got up and faced the company. "In general," she began at once, "I think we can pass the candidate completely on the psychological records. The Index of Subordination is low, but we don't want one too high for this post. Too, the Beta curve shows a good deal of variation, a Dionysian characteristic. There is, perhaps, a stronger sense of responsibility than is recorded in the Dionysian index, but this may not be a handicap."

"By no means," Hera said. "Responsibility is something we could all do with more of, around here." She shot a poisonous glance at Morpheus, whose eyes were now completely closed.

Forrester, busily wondering what his Beta curve was, and why it varied, and what he would do if he lost it and had to get another one, missed the next few words of Athena's report. The word that did impinge on his consciousness did so with a shock.

"Sex," Athena said. "But, after all, that is not quite in my department." She looked as if she were very glad of the fact. "In general, as I say, the psychological tests present no insuperable barriers."

"Fine," Hera said. She dug Zeus in the ribs again.

"Oh," Zeus said. "Yes. Fine."

"Next," Hera said.

"Yes," Zeus said. "By all means. Next."

Mars got up. He was now scratching the hair on his chest. He looked around at the others with a definitely unfriendly expression.

"The physical department is mine," he said. "The candidate can handle himself, all right. There isn't much doubt of it." He burped, wiped his mouth with the back of one hand, and went on: "Of course, he's let himself run to fat a little here and there, but it isn't really serious. Mainly a matter of glandular balance or something like that, as far as I understand Hermes' report."

Forrester began to feel like a prize chicken.

"And physical training," Mars said. "Well, there hasn't *been* any training, that's all. And that's bad."

"He is not being considered for your position," Vulcan said. "One muscular brainless imbecile is enough."

Mars took a deep breath.

"Please," Hera said. "Continue the report."

The breath came out in an explosion. "All right," Mars said. "Discounting the training end of things, and assuming that Hermes can fix up the glandular mess, I think he can pass the physical."

Forrester wasn't sure that he liked being referred to as a glandular mess. On the other hand, he asked himself, what could he do about it? He stood quietly, wondering what was coming next.

His worst fears were fulfilled.

Venus stepped forward and gave her report. Basically, it was a codicil, of a rather specialized nature, to the physical report. While it was going on, Forrester glanced at Athena. She looked every bit as embarrassed as he felt, and her face wore a look of sheer pain. Once he thought she was going to leave the room, but she remained grimly seated until it was all over.

Forrester couldn't figure out, when he thought about it, how the Gods had managed to give him all these tests without his knowing anything about it. But, then, they were supernatural, weren't they? And they had their own methods. A mortal didn't have to understand them.

Forrester wasn't sure he was happy with that idea, but he clung to it. It was the only one he had.

When Venus finished her report, there was a little silence.

"Any other comments?" Hera whispered to her husband.

"Ah, yes," Zeus said. "Other comments. If anyone has any other comments to make, please make them now. Now is the time to make them."

He sat back. Morpheus stirred slightly and spoke without opening his eyes or sitting up. "Sleep," he said.

Hera said: "Sleep?"

"Very important," Morpheus said slowly, "the candidate sleeps pretty well-soundly, as a matter of fact. The only trouble is that he doesn't get enough sleep. But then, no one on this entire crazy world ever does." He yawned and added: "Not even me."

Forrester passed a hand over his forehead. He realized, very suddenly, that he had come to a conclusion somewhere during the meeting. He was, he told himself, definitely sane.

That left another conclusion. He was not dreaming anything that was happening. It was all perfectly real.

And he was about to become a demi-God.

That in itself didn't sound so bad. But he began to wonder, in a quiet sort of way, just what was going to happen to William Forrester, acolyte and history professor, when Forrester/Bacchus had became a reality. With a blunt shock he knew that there was only one answer.

William Forrester was going to die.

It didn't matter what the verdict of the Gods was. There were more tests coming, he knew, and if he failed them the Gods would kill him quite literally and quite completely.

But, he went on, suppose he passed the tests.

In that case he was going to become Forrester/Bacchus, a substitute God. Plain old Bill Forrester would cease to exist entirely.

Oh, a few traces might remain-his Beta curve, for instance, whatever that was. But Bill Forrester would be gone. Somehow, the idea of a revenant Beta curve didn't make up for the basic loss.

On the other hand, he reminded himself again, what choice did he have?

None.

He forced himself to listen to what the Gods were saying.

Zeus cleared his throat. "Well, I think that closes the subject. Am I right, dear?"

"You are," Hera said.

"Very well," Zeus said. "Then the subject is closed, isn't it?"

Hera nodded wearily.

"In that case, we can proceed with the investiture. Hephaestus, will you please take charge of the candidate?"

Hephaestus/Vulcan sighed softly. "I suppose I must." He swung off the couch and stood half-crouched for a second. Forrester looked at him blankly. "Well," Vulcan said, "come on." He jerked his head toward Forrester. "Over here."

With one last backward glance at Venus, Forrester walked across the room. Vulcan turned and hobbled ahead of him toward the wall. Forrester followed until, almost at the wall, a Veil of Heaven appeared. Feeling almost used to the thing by now, Forrester followed Vulcan through, and he didn't even look behind him to see if the Veil had vanished after they'd come through. He knew perfectly well it had. It always did.

The room they had entered was similar to the others he had seen, but there was no change of colors. The walls glowed evenly and with a subdued light that filled the room evenly. And, for the first time, the walls weren't simply blanks that became things only when approached. The strangest-looking objects Forrester had ever seen filled benches, tables, chairs and the floor, and some were even tacked to the glowing walls. He stared at them for a long time.

No two were alike. They seemed to be all sizes, shapes and materials. The only thing they really had in common was that they were unrecognizable. They looked, Forrester thought, as if a truckload of non-objective twentieth-century sculpture had collided with another truck full of old television-set innards. Then, in some way, the two trucks had fallen in love and had children.

The scrambled horrors scattered throughout the room were, Forrester told himself bleakly, the children.

Vulcan sat down on the only empty chair with a sigh. "This is my workshop," he announced gravely. "It is not arranged for visitors, nor for the curious. I must advise you to touch nothing, if you wish to save your hands, your sanity, and very possibly your life."

Forrester nodded dumbly. Vulcan's tone hadn't been unfriendly; he had merely been warning a stranger, in the shortest and clearest manner possible, against the dangers of feeling the merchandise. Not, Forrester thought, that the warning was necessary. He would as soon have thought of trying to fly as he would of touching one of the mixed-up looking things.

"Now," Vulcan said, "if you'll —" He stopped. "Pardon me," he said, and levered himself upright. He went to a chair, swept a few constructions from it and put them carefully on a table. "Sit down," he said, motioning to the chair.

Gingerly, Forrester sat down.

Vulcan returned to his own chair and climbed onto it. "Now let us get to business."

"Business?" Forrester said.

"Oh, yes," Vulcan said. "I imagine you were pretty well bewildered for a while. No more than natural. But I think you've figured it out by now. You know you are going to be given the powers of a demi-God, don't you?"

"Yes. But —"

"Do not worry about it," Vulcan said. "The powers are simply powers. They are not burdens. At any rate, they will not be burdensome to you. We know that we have researched you to a fine point, as you may have gathered from the fol-de-rol back there." He gestured toward his right, evidently indicating the Court of the Gods.

"But," Forrester said, "suppose I'm not what your tests say. I mean, suppose I —"

"There is no need for supposition. Beyond any shadow of doubt, we know how you, as a mortal, will react to any conceivable set of circumstances."

"Oh," Forrester said. "But —"

"Precisely. You have realized what yet needs to be done. We know what your abilities and limitations are —as a mortal. The tests you have yet to pass are concerned with your actions and reactions as a demi-God."

Forrester swallowed hard. He felt as if he were on a moving roller-coaster. No matter how badly he wanted to get off, it was impossible to do so. He had to remain while the car hurtled on.

And where was he going?

The Gods, he told himself with more than ordinary meaning, knew.

"The power which is to be infused into you," Vulcan said, "if you don't mind the loose terminology —"

"I don't mind in the least," Forrester assured him earnestly. "Not in the least."

"The power infused into you will make some changes. These will not only be physical changes. Mental changes must be expected."

"Oh," Forrester said. "Mental changes."

"Correct. Physically, you see, you will become what no mortal can ever quite be: a perfectly functioning biological engine. Every sinew, nerve and muscle, every organ and gland, every tissue in your body will be in perfect harmonic balance with every other. Metabolically speaking, your catabolism and anabolism will be in such perfect balance that aging will not be possible."

Forrester thought that over. "I'll be immortal," he said.

"In that sense of the word," Vulcan said, "you will. You will be, as a matter of fact, quite a good deal tougher, stronger and harder than any animal now existing on the face of the Earth. I must except, of course, a few of the really big ones, like the elephant and the killer whale."

"Oh," Forrester said. "Sure."

"But make no mistake. You can still be killed. A bullet through the heart will not do the job; it will merely incapacitate you for a few hours. But if you were to have your head blown off by a grenade, you would be quite dead. Remember that."

"I don't see how I could forget it."

"You will heal with incredible rapidity, but there are limitations. Anything that pushes the balance too far will be fatal. You can lose a hand or even an arm without serious harm; the missing member will be regrown. But if you were to fall into a large meat-grinder —"

"I get the idea," Forrester said, feeling pale green.

"Good," Vulcan said. "However, there is more."

"More?"

"There are certain other powers to be given you in addition. You will learn of these later."

Forrester nodded blankly.

"Now," Vulcan said, "all these physical changes will have a definite effect upon your psychological outlook, as I imagine you can plainly see."

Forrester thought about it. "Well —"

"Let us suppose that you are a coward who has avoided fights all his life. Now you are given these powers. What will happen?"

"I'll be strong."

"Exactly. You will be strong. And because you are strong, and almost indestructible, you suddenly decide that you can now get your revenge on the people who have pushed you around."

"Well," Forrester said, "I —"

"You begin to look for fights," Vulcan said. "You go around beating up everyone you can find, simply because you now know you can get away with it. Do you understand me?"

"I guess so."

"A man with a vicious streak in him would be intolerable in this position. Can you see that? Take an example: Ares. Mars is a tough God, hard and at times brutal. But he is not vicious."

Forrester was a little surprised to hear Vulcan say anything nice about Mars. He knew, as everyone did, the long history of ill-will and positive hatred the two had built up between them. It had begun soon after Vulcan's marriage to Aphrodite/Venus.

He hadn't been a cripple then, of course. For a while, he and Venus had had a fine time. But Venus, apparently, just wasn't satisfied with the dull normal routine of married life. None of the Gods seemed to be, as a matter of fact. Either they were altogether too married, like Zeus, or else they weren't married enough, like Venus. Or else they were like Diana and Athena, indifferent to marriage.

At any rate, Venus had begun looking around for fresh talent. And the fresh talent had been right there ready to sign up for a long contract on a strictly extra-legal basis.

One day Vulcan caught them at it, his wife and Mars. Vulcan was angry, but Mars didn't exactly like to be interrupted, either, and he was a little faster on the draw. He tossed Vulcan over a nearby cliff, crippling him for good.

And as for Aphrodite-who knew? It was entirely possible that, by this time, the Goddess of Love had run through the entire list of Gods and was now at work on the mortals.

Forrester wasn't entirely sure he disliked the idea, on a simple physical level. But there was more than that to it, of course; there was Vulcan. Forrester found himself liking the solemn, positive workman. He didn't want to hurt him.

And a liaison with Venus was certain to do just that.

He came back to the present to hear Vulcan still discoursing. "Also," the God said, "changes in glandular balance must be made. These changes have a necessary effect on the brain. The personality changes subtly, though I can assure you that the change is not a marked one." He paused. "For all these reasons," he finished, "I am sure that you can see why we must subject you to further tests."

"I understand," Forrester said vaguely.

"Good. Now, you will not know whether a given incident-any given incident-is a perfectly natural occurrence or a test imposed on you by the Pantheon. Can you understand that?"

Forrester nodded.

Vulcan levered himself upright, his ugly face smiling just a little. "And remember what I have told you. No worrying. You don't even know just what any given test is supposed to accomplish, so you can't know whether the action you choose is right or wrong. Therefore, worrying will do nothing for you. You will be at your best if you simply behave naturally."

"I'll try."

"Remember, also, that you were picked not merely for your physical resemblance to Dionysus, but your psychological resemblance as well. Therefore, playing his part should be comparatively simple for you. Right?"

"I guess so," Forrester said, feeling both expectant and a little hopeless about it all.

"Fine," Vulcan said. "Now wait one moment." He turned and limped over to a structure that looked like a sort of worktable. When he came back, he was carrying several objects in his big hands. He selected one, an ovoid about the size of a marble, colored a dull orange, and handed it to Forrester. "Swallow that."

Forrester took it cautiously. As soon as he found out what he was supposed to do with the thing, its dimensions seemed to grow. It looked about the size of a golf ball in his shaking hands.

"Swallow it?" he said tentatively.

"Correct," Vulcan said.

"But —"

"This object is a —well, call it a talisman. It will not dissolve, and it is recoverable, but for the Investiture it must be inside you."

"But —"

"You will find it so easy to swallow that you will need no water. Go ahead."

Forrester put the thing in his mouth and swallowed once, just to test Vulcan's statement. The effect was surprising. He could barely feel it leave his tongue, and he couldn't feel it go down at all. He swallowed again, experimentally, and explored the inside of his mouth with his tongue.

"It is gone," Vulcan said. "Good."

"It's gone, all right," Forrester said wonderingly.

"The sandals are next." Vulcan selected a pair of sandals with rather thick soles and handed them over. They were apparently made of gold. Forrester obediently strapped them on, and Vulcan next handed him a pair of golden cylinders indented to fit his curved fingers.

46

"You hold these very tightly," Vulcan said. "During the Investiture, you must grip them as hard as you can." He peered closely at them and pointed to one. "This one goes in the left hand. The other goes in the right. Squeeze them as if-as if you were trying to crush them. All right?"

"All right," Forrester said.

Vulcan nodded. "Good. From this moment on, do exactly as you are told. Answer questions truthfully. Keep nothing secret. Remember my instructions."

"Right," Forrester said doubtfully.

"Come on," Vulcan said, heading for the wall. The inevitable Veil of Heaven appeared, and Forrester followed through it as before.

The room they entered was not, he thought, the same one they had been in before. Or, if it was, it had changed a great deal. It was difficult to tell anything for sure; the shifting walls looked the same, but they also looked like the shifting walls in Venus' apartments.

At any rate, there were now no couches on the floor. The room seemed even bigger than before, and when the walls settled down to a steady golden glow, Forrester felt lost in the immensity of the place. In the center of the room was a raised golden dais. It was about five feet across and nearly three feet high.

The Gods were ranged around it in a semicircle, facing him. Vulcan slipped into an empty space in the line, and Forrester stood perfectly alone, holding the cylinders.

Zeus cleared his throat. "Step up on the dais," he said.

Stumbling slightly, Forrester managed to do so without losing his grip on the cylinders.

In the center of the raised platform, with the Gods staring at him, he felt like something under a microscope.

"William Forrester," Zeus said, and he shuddered. The All-Father's voice had never been more powerful. "William Forrester, from this moment onward you will renounce your present name. You will be known as Dionysus the Lesser until and unless it shall please us to confer another name on you. Henceforth, you will be, in part, a recipient of the worship due to Dionysus, and you will hold the rank of demi-God. Do you accept these judgments and this honor?"

Forrester gulped. A long time seemed to pass. At last he found his voice. "I do," he said.

"Very well," Zeus said.

The Gods joined hands and closed the circle around Forrester, surrounding him completely. The golden auras that shone about their bodies grew more and more bright. Forrester clutched the golden cylinders tightly.

Then, very suddenly, there was an explosion of light. Forrester thought he had staggered, but he was never sure. Everything was too bright to see. Dizziness began, and grew.

The room whirled and tipped. Somewhere a great organlike note began, and went on and on.

Forrester convulsed with the force of a single great burst of energy that crashed through his nervous system.

And then, in a timeless instant, everything went black.

CHAPTER 7

The morning of the Autumn Bacchanal dawned bright and clear-thanks to the intervention of the Pantheon. In New York, the leaves were only just beginning to turn, and the sun was still high enough in the sky to make the afternoons warm and pleasant. Zeus All-Father had promised good weather for the festival, and a strong, warm wind from the Gulf of Mexico was moving out the crisp autumn air before the sun had risen an hour above the horizon.

The practicing that had gone on in thousands of homes throughout the city was at an end. The Autumn Bacchanal was here at last, and the Beginning Service, which had started in the little Temple-on-the-Green right at dawn, when the sun's rays had first touched the tops of New York's towers, was approaching its end. The people clustered in the building, and the incomparably greater number scattered outside it, were feeling the first itch of restlessness.

Soon the Grand Procession would begin, starting as always from the Temple-on-the-Green and wending its slow way northward to the upper end of Central Park at 110th Street. Then the string of worshippers would turn and head back for the Temple at the lower end of the Park, with fanfare and pageantry on a scale calculated to do honor to the God of the festival, to outshine not only every other festival, but every past year of the Autumn Bacchanal itself.

The Autumn Bacchanal was devoted to the celebration of the harvest, and more specifically the harvest and processing of the grape. All the wineries for hundreds of miles around had shipped hogshead after hogshead and barrel after barrel of fine wine-red, white, rose, still, or sparkling-as joyous sacrifice to Dionysus/Bacchus, and in thanks that the fertility rites of the Vernal Bacchanal had brought them good crops. Wine flowed from everywhere into the city, and now the immense reserves were stacked away, awaiting the revels. Even the brewers and distillers had sent along their wares, from the mildest beer to vodka of 120 proof, joining unselfishly in the celebration even though, technically, they were not under Dionysian protection at all, but were the wards of Ceres, the Goddess of grain.

Celebrants, liquors, chants, preparations, balloons, confetti, edibles and all the other appurtenances of the festival spiraled dizzyingly upward, reaching proportions unheard of throughout history. And, in a back room at the Temple-on-the-Green, the late William Forrester sat, trying to forget all about them, and suffering from a continuous case of nerves.

Diana marched up and down in front of him, smacking her left fist into her calloused little right palm. "Now listen," she said crisply. "I know you're all hot and bothered, kid, but there's no reason to be. You're doing fine. They love you out there."

"Sure I am," Forrester said, unconvinced.

"Well, you are," Diana said. "You just got to have confidence, that's all. Keep your spirits up. Tried singing?"

"Singing?"

"Singing, kid. Raises the spirits."

Forrester blinked. "Really?"

"Take it from me," Diana said. "How about Tenting Tonight?"

"How about what?"

"Tenting Tonight," Diana said. "You know."

"I —guess I do." Forrester wished that Diana would do more than treat him like a pal. She was a remarkably beautiful woman, if you liked the type, and Forrester liked virtually any type.

Now, success appeared to be within his grasp. But it did seem an odd time to bring the subject up. Oh, well, he thought, maybe she was just trying to cheer him up and had picked this way of doing it.

It worked, too, he told himself happily.

He cleared his throat. "Where?"

Diana stared. "Where?"

"That's right," Forrester said. Something was going wrong but he couldn't discover what it was. "The tenting."

"Oh," Diana said. "Right here. Now. Raises the spirits."

"I should say it does!" Forrester agreed enthusiastically. "But after all-right here —"

"Don't worry about it, kid. Nobody will hear you."

"*Hear* me?"

"Anyway, it's nothing to be ashamed of. Lots of people do it when they feel low."

"I'll bet they do," Forrester said. "But it's different with you and me."

"Me?" Diana said. "What do I have to do with it? I just told you —"

"Well, sure. And here and now is as good a time and place as any."

Diana stepped back a pace. "Okay, let's hear it. Sing!"

"Sing? You mean I have to sing for my —"

"I'll join you," Diana said.

Forrester nodded. He was beginning to get confused. "You'd better," he said.

"*Tenting tonight on the old camp grounds,*" she sang. "Now come on."

Forrester coughed. "Oh," he said. "Sing."

"Sure," Diana said, and they went through the song together. "How about another chorus?" she asked.

"It's all right, Diana," Forrester said, knowing she preferred the name to her Greek one of Artemis. "I feel fine now."

"Well," Diana said in a disappointed voice, "all right."

What surprised Forrester most was that he *did* feel fine. All the Gods had helped him in the past several months, but Diana had been especially helpful. As a forest Goddess, and as Protectress of the Night, she'd been able to tell him a lot about how an orgy was arranged. He had often wished that she would teach by example, but now, he discovered, it was too late for wishing.

She was, he told himself with only faint regret, just like a sister to him. Or even a brother.

"I guess everything will be okay," he said. "Won't it?"

Diana clapped him on the back. "You're going to be great. Just go out there and show 'em what kind of a God you are."

"But what kind of a God am I?"

"Just keep cool, kid. You won't fail me —I know it."

"I'll try," Forrester said. "Only I'm getting nervous just sitting around here. I wish we could go out and stroll around; we've got plenty of time, anyhow."

Diana nodded. "It's ten minutes yet before the Procession starts. I suppose we might as well take a look around, kid, if it makes you feel better."

"It might."

"Fine, then. But how do you want to go?"

Forrester blinked. "How?"

"Invisibility," Diana said, "or incognito?"

"Oh," Forrester said. Then he added: "You're asking me?"

"Of course I am, kid. Now, look: this is your celebration, remember? You're Dionysus. Got it? Even in my presence, you act the part now. You ought to know that."

"Well, sure, but —"

"Keep this in mind. These people haven't had a Sabbatical Bacchanal in seven years. Every seven years they get to see their God-and this year you're it. Right?"

"I guess so. But —"

"No buts," Diana said. "You're the boss and they're your worshippers. That's all there is to it. Now, you've got to make up your mind. What'll it be?"

Forrester thought. "Well," he said at last, "I guess it had better be incognito. With this crowd, there's too much likelihood of getting bumped into if we're invisible. Right?"

Diana grinned. "That's the boy! You're thinking straight now!"

Forrester had the sudden feeling that he had just passed another test. But he didn't quite dare ask about it "All right," he said instead. "Let's go."

He put his mind to work concentrating on the special faculties that his demi-God power gave him. His face began to change. He looked less and less like Dionysus as the seconds went by, and more and more like William Forrester. At the same time, the golden aura around his body began to fade. After a few minutes he looked like William Forrester completely, a nice enough guy but pretty much of a nonentity.

Diana, with the greater power of a true Goddess, achieved the same sort of result almost instantly. Her aura was gone and the sparkle had left her eyes. Her brown hair looked a little mousy now, and her face was merely pretty instead of being gloriously beautiful.

"Just one thing," Forrester said. "We'd better make ourselves invisible just to leave the Temple. Somebody might suspect we weren't ordinary people at all."

"Right again," Diana smiled. She nodded her head and blinked out.

Forrester could still see a cloudy outline of her in the room, but he knew that was because he was a demi-God, with special powers. An ordinary mortal, he knew, would see nothing at all.

He followed her into invisibility and walked out the back door of the Temple-on-the-Green. The door was open and two Temple Myrmidons, wearing the golden grape-clusters of Dionysus on their shoulder patches, stood outside the door. Neither of them saw Forrester and Diana leave.

Three minutes later, they were standing near the doorway of the Temple, watching the preparations for the Grand Procession. The fifty priests of Dionysus gathered there while the enormous crowd pushed and shoved to get a better view of the ritual. The sacrifice of the first fruits had been completed, and now, at the door of the Temple, each of the fifty priests filled a chalice from a huge hogshead of purple wine.

They chanted a prayer in unison and spilled half the wine on the ground as a libation. Then they lifted the chalices to their lips and drank, finishing the other half in one long motion.

The chalices were set down, and a cheer rose from the crowd.

The Bacchanal had begun!

The priests separated into two equal groups. Twenty-five of them started northward, marching to their positions at regularly spaced intervals in the procession. The remaining twenty-five stayed behind, ready to accompany Dionysus himself at the tail of the parade.

Each of the other Gods was represented by a special detachment of ten Myrmidons, each contingent wearing the distinctive shoulder patch of the God it served: the thunderbolt of Zeus, the blazing sun of Apollo, the pipes of Pan, the sword of Mars, the hammer of Vulcan, the poppy of Morpheus, the winged foot of Mercury, the trident of Neptune, the cerberus of Pluto, the peacock of Hera, the owl of Athena, the dove of Venus, the crescent of Diana, and the sprig of wheat that represented Mother Ceres. The Myrmidons grinned in expectation of the good times coming; a Dionysian festival was always something special, and competition for the contingents was always tough.

There were balloons everywhere, as the crowd shoved and pushed into the line of march. Someone was bawling an old song about the lack of liquor, and the strident voice carried over the shouts and halloos of the mob:

"How dry I am —"

Forrester and Diana, now visible, pushed their way through the crowds. A man flung his arm around the Goddess with abandon, shouting something indistinguishable; Diana shook him off gently and went on. Forrester almost tripped over a small boy sitting on the grass and crying. A Myrmidon was standing over him, and the child's mother was trying to lift the boy.

"I wanna go to the orgy," the boy kept saying. "I wanna go to the orgy."

"Next year," the mother told him. "Next year, child, when you're six."

The Myrmidon lifted the child and carried him away. The mother shouted an address after him, and the Myrmidon nodded, pushed his way through a gesticulating group of celebrants and disappeared in the direction of Central Park West. There, other Dionysian Myrmidons were patrolling, making sure that no non-Dionysian got in except by special invitation. Any non-Dionysian who wanted to celebrate was supposed to do it on the streets of the city, and not in Central Park, which was going to be crowded enough with legitimate revelers.

The shouting and screaming went on, people pushing and shoving, confetti beginning to drift like a light snow over the worshippers. One man held five balloons and a cigarette, and he was popping the balloons with the cigarette tip, one by one. Every time one of the balloons exploded, a group of women and girls around him shrieked and laughed.

Forrester turned back. Behind a convenient bush, he and Diana made themselves invisible again, and re-entered the Temple-on-the-Green.

The silence inside the Temple was deafening.

"The noise out there could break eardrums," Forrester complained. "I've never heard anything like it."

"Just wait," Diana told him. "The music will start any time now-and then you'll *really* hear something." She paused. "Ready?"

Forrester glanced down at himself. "I guess so. How do I look?" He had constructed a golden *chiton* and mentally clothed himself in it. It was covered by a grape-purple cloak embroidered with golden grapevines. And around his head a circlet of woven grapevines had appeared, made of solid gold. It was a little heavier than Forrester had expected it would be, but it lent him, he thought, rather a dashing air.

"Great," Diana said. "Just great."

"Think so?" Forrester said, feeling rather pleased.

"Sure you do. Now go out there and give 'em the old college try."

Forrester gulped. "How about you?"

"Me? I'm on my way out of here. This is your show, kid. Make the most of it."

Forrester watched her go out the rear door. He was alone. And the Autumn Bacchanal Processional was about to begin.

CHAPTER 8

Noise! Forrester, seated in the great golden palanquin supported by twelve hefty Priests of Dionysus, had never seen or heard anything like it. He waited there on the steps of the little Temple-on-the-Green for the Procession to wind by, so that he could take his place at the end of it. But the Procession looked endless.

First came a corps of Priests and Myrmidons, leading their way stolidly through the paths of Central Park. Following them came the revelers, a mass of men and women marching, laughing, singing, shouting, dancing their way along to the accompaniment of more music than Forrester had ever dreamed of.

The Dionysians had practiced for months, and almost everything was represented. There were violinists prancing along, violists and a crew of long-haired gentlemen and ladies playing the viol da gamba and the viol d'amore; there were guitarists plunking madly away, banjo players strumming and ukelele addicts picking at their strings, somehow all chorusing together. In a special pair of floats there were bass players, bass fiddle players and cellists, jammed tightly together and somehow managing to draw enormous sounds and scratches out of the big instruments. And behind them came the main band of musicians.

The woodwinds followed: piccolo players piping, flutists fluting, oboe players, red-cheeked and glassy-eyed, concentrating on making the most piercing possible sounds, men playing English horns, clarinets, bass clarinets, bassoons and contra-bassoons, along with men playing serpents and, behind them, a dancing group fingering ocarinas and adding their bit to the general tumult, and two women tootling madly away on hoarse-sounding zootibars.

And then, near the center of the musicians, were the brass: trumpets and trumpets-a-piston, trombones and valve trombones and Fulk horns, all blatting away to split the sky with maddening sound, Sousaphones and saxophones and French horns and bass horns and hunting horns, and tubas along in their own little cart, six round-cheeked men lost in the curves of the great instruments, valiantly blowing away as they rolled by into the woods of the park, making the city itself resound with tremendous noise and shattering cadence. And behind them was the battery.

Kettle drums, bass drums, xylophones, Chinese gongs, vibraphones, snare drums and high-hat cymbals paraded by in carts, banged and stroked and tinkled enthusiastically by crew after crew of maddened tympanists. And then came the others, on foot: tambourines and wood blocks and parade cymbals and castanets. At the tail of this portion of the Procession came a single old man wearing spectacles and riding in a small cart drawn by a donkey. He had white hair and he was playing on a series of water-glasses filled to various levels. His ear was cocked toward the glasses with painstaking care. He was entirely inaudible in the general din, but he looked happy and satisfied; he was doing his bit.

After him followed a group of entirely naked men and women playing sackbuts, and another group playing recorders. Bringing up the rear, as the Procession curved, was a magnificent aggregation of men and women yowling away on bagpipes of all shapes and sizes. All of the men wore sporrans and nothing more; the women wore nothing at all. The music that emanated from this group was enough to unhinge the mind.

And then came the keyboard instruments, into the middle of which the five theremin-players had been stuck for no reason at all. The strange howls of this unearthly instrument filtered through the sound of pianos, harpsichords, psalters, clavichords, virginals and three gigantic electric organs pumping at full strength.

And bringing up the very rear of the Procession was a special decorated cart, full of color and holding a lone man with long white hair, wearing a rusty black suit and playing away, with great attention and care, on the largest steam calliope Forrester had ever met. Jets of steam fizzed out of the top, and music bawled from the interior of the massive thing as it went by, trailing the Procession into the woods, and the entire aggregation swung into a single song, hundred upon hundreds of musicians and singers all coming down hard on the opening strains of the Hymn to Dionysus:

"Mine eyes have seen the glory of the Lord who rules the wine —

He has trampled out the vintage of the grapes upon the vine!"

The twelve Priests picked up the palanquin and Forrester adjusted his weight so they wouldn't find it too heavy. It was impossible to think in the mass of noise and music that went on and on, as the Procession wound uptown through the paths of Central Park, and the musicians banged and scraped and blew and pounded and stroked and plucked, and the great Hymn rose into the air, filling the entire city with the bawled chorus as even the twelve Priests joined in, adding to the ear-splitting din:

"Glory, Glory, Dionysus!

Glory, Glory, Dionysus!

Glory, Glory, Dionysus!

While his wine goes flowing on!"

Forrester had always been disturbed by what he thought might have been a double meaning in that last line, but it didn't disturb him now. Nothing seemed to disturb him as the Procession wound on, and he was laughing uproariously and winking and nodding at his worshippers as they sang and played all around him, and the hours went by. Halfway there, he fished in the air and brought down the small golden disks with the picture of Dionysus on them that were a regular feature of the Processional, and flung them happily into the crowd ahead.

Only one was allowed per person, so there was not much scrambling, but some of the coins pattered down on the various instruments, and one landed in the old gentleman's middle-C water glass and had to be fished out before he could go on with the Hymn.

Carousing and noisy, the Procession finally reached the huge stand at the far end of the park, and the music stopped. On the stand was a whole new group of musicians: harpists, lyrists, players of the flageolet and dulcimer, two men sweating over glockenspiels, a group equipped with zithers and citharas and sitars, three women playing nose-flutes, two men with shofars, and a tall, blond man playing a clarino trumpet. As the Procession ground to a halt, this new band struck up the Hymn again, played it through twice, and then stopped.

Seven girls filed out onto the platform in front of the musicians. One was there representing every year since the last Sabbatical Bacchanal. Forrester, riding high on the palanquin, beamed down at them, roaring with happy laughter. They were all for him. Having been carried to one end of the park in triumph, he was now to march back at the head of his people, surrounded by seven of the most beautiful girls in New York.

Their final selection had been left, he knew, to a brewery which had experience in these matters. And the girls certainly looked like the pick of anybody's crop. Forrester beamed at them again, stood up in the palanquin and spread his arms wide.

Then he sprang. In a flying leap, he went high into the air and did a full somersault, landing on his toes on the stage, twenty-five feet away. The girls were kneeling in a circle around him.

"Come, my doves!" he bellowed. "Come, my pigeons!" His Godlike golden baritone carried for blocks.

He grabbed the two nearest girls by their hands and helped them to their feet. They blushed and lowered their eyes.

"Come, all of you!" Forrester shouted. "We are about to begin the revels!"

The girls rose and Forrester gestured them in closer. Then, surrounded by all seven, he threw back his head again.

"A revel to make history!" he roared. "A revel beyond the imagination of man! A revel fit for your God!"

The crowd cheered wildly. Forrester picked up one of the girls, tossed her into the air and caught her easily as she descended. He set her on her feet and put his hands solidly on his hips.

"My cup!" he shouted. "Fill you my cup!"

Behind the stage was a corps of Priests guarding a mountainous golden hogshead of wine, adjudged the finest wine produced during the year.

"We shall have drink!" Forrester shouted. "We shall let the revels roar on!"

Two priests came forward, staggering under the weight of a gigantic crystal goblet containing fully two gallons of the clear purple liquid. They bore it to Forrester with great pomp, and before them came a dozen players on the gahoon and the contra-gahoon, making Forrester's ears ring with deafening fanfares.

Forrester took the great goblet in one hand and held it with ease. Then he lifted it into the air with a wordless shout, filled his lungs and laughed. He put the goblet to his lips and drained it in a single long motion. A mighty hurrah shook the trees and rocks of the park.

Forrester waved the goblet. "Again. Fill you my cup once more!" He embraced the seven girls with one sweeping gesture of his arms. "My little beauties must have drink! Fill you the cup!"

He passed it back to the Priests carefully. They received it and went back to where the others were waiting to fill it. Then they staggered forward again and Forrester picked up the brimming goblet. He held it for the girls, each of whom tried to outdrink the others. But it was still more than half-full when they were finished.

Forrester raised it again. The crowd shouted. "Observe your God!" Forrester roared. "Observe his powers!" He threw his head back and emptied the goblet. Then, holding it in one hand, he faced the assemblage and delivered himself of one Godlike belch.

The crowd shrieked its approval. Forrester had the goblet filled once more and put three of the girls in charge of it. Then he came down the steps from the platform and began the long march back to the Temple-on-the-Green.

The shouting, carousing revelers followed him joyfully. Halfway back, one of them stumbled forward and caught at the trailing edge of his robe. There was an immediate crackle and burst of static electricity, and the stumbler fell back yelping and shaking his arms. The Myrmidons came and took him away.

Dionysus couldn't be touched by anyone except those authorized to do so-the seven girls and the Priests. But Forrester barely noticed the accident; he was too happy on top of his world, laughing and hugging the girls close to him.

Behind him, the Priests at the golden hogshead, now set free to taste the wine themselves, had lost no time. They were dipping in busily with their own goblets —a good deal smaller than the two-gallon crystal one for Dionysus himself. There was not even any need for libations; enough ran over the brimming edges of the goblets to take care of that detail, and the Priests were soon well on the way to becoming sozzled.

The musicians, now joined by the corps which had waited on the uptown stage, struck up a new tune, and drowned out even the shouting crowds as they cheered their God. After a little while, the crowds began to sing along with the magnificent noise:

"*Dionysus wrapped his hand around the goblet,*

Around the goblet-around the goblet —

Dionysus wrapped his hand around the goblet,

And we'll all get-stinking drunk!"

It was by no means an official hymn, but Forrester didn't mind; it was sung with such a great deal of honest enthusiasm. He himself did not join in the singing; he was otherwise occupied. With his arms around two of the girls, drinking now and then from the great goblet three more were holding, and winking and laughing at the extra two, he made his joyous way down the petal-strewn paths of Central Park.

The Procession wound down through the paths, over bridges and under tunnels, singing and playing and marching and dancing madly, while Forrester, at its head, caroused as merrily as any four of them. They reached a bridge crossing a little stream and Forrester sprang at it with a great somersaulting leap that carried the two girls he was holding right along with him. He set them down at the slope of the bridge, laughing and giggling and the other girls, with the Procession behind them, soon caught up. Forrester let go of one of the girls, grabbed the goblet with his free hand and swung it in a magnificent gesture.

"Forward!" he cried.

The Procession surged over the bridge, Forrester at its head. He grabbed the girl again, handing the goblet back to his corps of three carriers, and bowed and grinned at his worshippers behind him, surging forward, and at some others standing under the bridge, ankle-deep, shin-deep, even knee-deep in the rushing water, craning their necks upward to get a really good view of their God as he passed over. There were over a hundred of them there.

Forrester didn't see a hundred of them.

He saw one of them first, and then two more. And time seemed to stop with a grinding halt. Forrester wanted to run and hide. He clutched the girls closer to him with one instinctive gesture, and then realized he'd made the wrong move. But it was too late. He was lost, he told himself dolefully. The sun had gone out, the wine had lost its power and the celebration had degenerated to a succession of ugly noises.

The first face he saw belonged to Gerda Symes.

In that timeless instant, Forrester felt that he could see every detail of the soft, small face, the dark hair, the slim, curved figure. She was smiling up at him, but her face looked a little bewildered, as if she were smiling only because it was the thing to do. Forrester wondered, panic-stricken, how she, an Athenan, had managed to get entry to a Dionysian revel-but his wonder only lasted for a second. Then he saw the second and third faces, and he knew.

The second face belonged to an absolute stranger. He looked like an oafish clod, even viewed objectively, and Forrester was making no efforts in that direction. He had one arm around Gerda's waist and he was grinning up at her, and, sideways, at Forrester with a look that made them co-conspirators in what was certainly planned to be Gerda's seduction. Forrester didn't like the idea. As a matter of fact, he hated it more than he could possibly say.

But all he could do was trust to Gerda's own doubtless sterling good sense. She couldn't possibly prefer a lout like her current escort to good old Bill Forrester, could she?

On the other hand, she thought Bill Forrester was dead. She'd had to think that; when he became Dionysus the Lesser, he couldn't just disappear. He had to die officially-and, as far as Gerda knew, the death wasn't just an official formality.

With Bill Forrester dead, then, had she turned to the oaf for comfort? He didn't look very comforting, Forrester thought. He looked like a damned outrage on the face of the Earth. Forrester disliked him on first sight, and knew perfectly well that any future sights would only increase the dislike.

It was the third face, though that explained everything.

The third face was as unmistakable as Gerda's, though in an entirely different way. It was fleshy and pasty, and it belonged, of course, to Gerda's lovable brother Ed. Forrester saw everything in one flash of understanding.

Ed Symes obviously had enough pull to get his sister invited to the Bacchanal. And from the looks of Gerda, he hadn't let the matter rest there. She was holding a half-filled plastic mug of wine in one hand —a mug with the picture of Dionysus stamped on it, which for some reason increased Forrester's outrage-and she was trying her best to look as if she were reveling.

From the looks of her, Ed had managed to get her about eight inches this side of half-pickled. And from the horribly cheerful look on Ed's countenance, he wasn't about to stop at the half-pickled mark, either.

Of course, from Ed's point of view-and Forrester told himself sternly that he had to be fair about this whole thing-from Ed's point of view there was nothing wrong in what was happening. He wanted to cheer Gerda up (undoubtedly the news of the Forrester demise had been quite a shock to her, poor girl), and what better way than to introduce her to his own religion, the best of all possible religions? The Autumn Bacchanal must have looked like the perfect time and place for that introduction, and Gerda's escort, a friend of Ed's —somehow Forrester had to think of him as Ed's friend; it was clearly not possible that he was Gerda's —had been brought along to help cheer the girl up and show her the advantages of worshipping Dionysus.

Unfortunately, the advantages hadn't turned out to be all that had been expected of them. Because now Gerda had seen Forrester alive and —

Wait a minute, Forrester told himself.

Gerda hadn't seen William Forrester at all.

She had seen just what she expected to see; Dionysus, God of Wine. There was no reason for him to shrink from her, or try to hide. Just because he was walking along with seven beautiful girls, drinking about sixteen times the consumption of any normal right-thinking fish, and carousing like the most unprincipled of men, he didn't have to be ashamed of himself.

He was only doing his job.

And Gerda did not know that he wasn't Dionysus.

The thought made him feel a little better, but it saddened him, too, just a bit. He set himself grimly and shouted: "Forward!" once more. To his own ears, his voice lacked conviction, but the crowd didn't seem to notice. The cheered frantically. Forrester wished they would all go away.

He started forward. His foot found a large pebble that hadn't been there before, and he performed the magnificent feat of tripping on it. He flailed the air frantically, and managed to regain his balance. Then he was back on his feet, clutching at the girls. His big left toe hurt, but he ignored the agony bravely.

He had to think of something to do, and fast. The crowd had seen him stumble-and that just didn't happen to a God. It wouldn't have happened to him, either except for Gerda.

He got his mind off Gerda with an effort and thought about what to do to cover his slip. In a moment he had it. He swore a great oath, empurpling the air. Then he bent down and picked up the stone. He held it aloft for a second, and then threw it. Slowly and carefully he pointed his index finger at it, extending it and raising his thumb like a little boy playing Stick-'Em-Up.

"Zap," he said mildly, cocking the thumb forward.

A crackling, searing bolt of blue-white energy leaped out of the tip of his index finger in a pencil-thin beam. It sped toward the falling pebble, speared it and wrapped it in coruscating splendor. Then the pebble exploded, scattering into a fine display of flying dust.

The crowd stopped moving and singing immediately.

Only the musicians, too intent on their noisemaking to see what had gone on, went on playing. But the crowd, having seen Forrester's display and heard his oath, was as silent as a collection of statues. When a God became angry, each was obviously thinking, there was absolutely no telling what was going to happen. Foxholes, some of them might have told themselves, would definitely be a good idea. But, of course, there weren't any foxholes in Central Park. There was nothing to do but stand very still, and hope you weren't noticed, and hope for the best.

Even Gerda, Forrester saw, had stopped, her face still, her hand lifted in a half-finished wave, the plastic cup forgotten.

I've got to do something, Forrester thought. *I can't let this kind of thing go on.*

He thought fast, spun around and pointed directly at Ed Symes, standing in the water below the bridge.

"You, there!" he bellowed.

Symes turned a delicate fish-belly white. Against this basic color, his pimples stood out strongly, making, Forrester thought, a rather unusual and somewhat striking effect. The man looked as if he wished he could sink out of sight in the ankle-deep water.

His mouth opened two or three times. Forrester waited, getting a good deal of pleasure out of the simple sight. Finally Symes spoke. "Me?"

"Certainly you! You look like a tough young specimen."

Symes tried to grin. The effect was ghastly. "I do?" He said tentatively.

"Of course you do. Your God tells you so. Do you doubt him?"

"Doubt? No. Absolutely not. Never. Wouldn't think of it. Tough young specimen. That's what I am. Tough. And young. Tough young specimen. Certainly. You bet."

"Good," Forrester said. "Now let's see you in action."

Symes took a deep breath. He seemed to be savoring it, as if he thought it was going to be his very last. "Wh-what do you want me to do?"

"I want you to pick up another stone and throw it. Let's see how high you can get it."

Symes was obviously afraid to move from his spot in the water. Instead of going back to the land, he fished around near his feet and finally managed to come up with a pebble almost as big as his fist. He looked at it doubtfully.

"Throw!" Forrester said in a voice like thunder.

Symes, galvanized, threw. It flew up in the air. Forrester drew a careful bead on it, went *zap* again with the pointed finger, and blasted the rock into dust.

The silence hung on.

Forrester laughed. "Not a bad throw for a mortal! And a good trick, too —a fine display!" He faced the crowd. "Now, there-what do you say to the entertainment your God provides? Wasn't that *fun?*"

Well, naturally it was, if Dionysus said so. A great trick, as a matter of fact. And a perfectly wonderful display. The crowd agreed immediately, giving a long rousing cheer. Forrester waved at them, and then turned to a squad of Myrmidons standing nearby.

"Go to that man and his friends!" he shouted, noticing that Symes's knees had begun to shake.

The Myrmidons obeyed.

"See that they follow near me. Allow them to remain close to me at all times —I may need a good stone-thrower later!"

Gerda, her brother and the oaf without a name were rounded up in a hurry, and soon found themselves being hustled along, willy-nilly, out of the water, up onto the bridge and into Dionysus' van, where they followed in the wake of the God, in front of the rest of the Procession. Of the three, Forrester noted, Gerda was the only one who didn't seem to think the invitation a high honor. The sight gave him a kind of hope.

And at least, he thought, *I can keep an eye on her this way.*

The Procession wended its way on, bending slowly southward toward the little Temple-on-the-Green again. The musicians played energetically, switching now from the hymn to their unofficial little ditty. Some switched before others, some switched after, and some never bothered to switch at all. The battery, caught between the opposing claims of two perfectly good songs and a lot of extraneous matter, filled in as best they could with a good deal of forceful banging and pounding, aided by the steam calliope, and the result of all effort was a growing cacophony that should have been terribly unpleasant but somehow wasn't.

The shouting of the crowd, joking and singing, may have had something to do with it; nothing was clearly distinguishable, but the general feeling was that a lot of noise was being produced, and that was all to the good. Noise could have been packaged by the board foot and sold in quantities sufficient to equip every town meeting throughout the country in full for seven years, and there would have been enough left over, Forrester thought, to provide for the subways, the classrooms, the offices and even a couple of really top-grade traffic jams.

Gerda and the others of her party marched quietly. Ed, Forrester noticed, tried a few cheers, but he got cold stares from his sister and soon desisted. The oaf shambled along, his arm no longer around Gerda's waist. This pleased Forrester no end, and he was in quite a happy mood by the time the Procession reached the Temple-on-the-Green.

He was so happy that he performed his atoning high jump once again, this time with a double somersault and a jack-knife thrown in, just to make things interesting, and landed gently, feeling positively exhilarated and very Godlike, on the roof of the Temple.

As the Procession straggled in, the music stopped. Forrester cleared his throat and shouted in his most penetrating roar to the silent assemblage: "Hear me!"

The crowd stirred, looked up and paid him the most rapt attention.

"On with the revels!" he roared. "Let the dancing begin! Let my wine flow like the streams of the park! Let joy be unrestrained!"

He stood on the roof then, watching the crowd begin to disperse. It was the middle of the afternoon, and Forrester was amazed at how quickly the time had passed. The Procession itself had taken a good six hours from start to finish, now that he looked back on it, but it certainly hadn't seemed so long. And he didn't even feel tired, in spite of all the dancing and cavorting he had gone in for.

He did feel slightly intoxicated, but he wasn't sure how much of that feeling was due purely and simply to the liquor he had managed to consume. But otherwise, he told himself, he felt perfectly fine.

The musicians were breaking up into little groups of three and four and five and going off to play softly to themselves among the trees. The man with the steam calliope sat exhausted over his keyboard. The old man with the water glasses was receiving the earnest congratulations of a lot of people who looked like relatives. And now that the official music-making was over, a lot of amateurs playing jews'-harps and tissue-paper-covered combs and slide-whistles had broken out their contraptions and were gaily making a joyful noise unto their God. If, Forrester thought, you wanted to call it joyful. The general tenor of the sound was a kind of swooping, batlike whine.

Forrester stared down. There were Gerda and her brother and the oaf. They were standing close by the Temple, three Myrmidons keeping guard over them. The rest of the crowd had dissolved into little bunches spreading all over the park. Forrester knew he would have to leave, too, and very soon. There were seven girls waiting for him down below.

Not that he minded the idea. Seven beautiful girls, after all, were seven beautiful girls. But he did want to keep an eye on Gerda, and he wasn't sure whether he would be able to do it when he got busy.

Somewhere in the bushes, someone began to play a kazoo, adding the final touch of melancholy and heartbreak to the music. The formal and official part of the Bacchanal was now over.

The *real* fun, Forrester thought dismally, was about to begin.

CHAPTER 9

"Now," Forrester said gaily, "let's see if your God has all the names right, shall we?"

The seven girls seated around him in a half-circle on the grass giggled. One of them simpered.

"Hmm," Forrester said. He pointed a finger. "Dorothy," he said. The finger moved. "Judy. Uh-Bette. Millicent. Jayne." He winked at the last two. They had been his closest companions on the march down. "Beverly," he said, "and Kathy. Right?"

The girls laughed, nodding their heads. "You can call me Millie," Millicent said.

"All right, Millie." For some reason this drew another big laugh. Forrester didn't know why, but then, he didn't much care, either. "That's fine," he said. "Just fine."

He gave all the girls a big, wide grin. It looked perfectly convincing to them, he was sure, but there was one person it didn't convince: Forrester. He knew just how far from a grin he felt.

As a matter of fact, he told himself, he was in something of a quandary.

He was not exactly inexperienced in the art of making love to beautiful young women. After the last few months, he was about as experienced as he could stand being. But his education had, it now appeared, missed one vital little factor.

He was used to making love to a beautiful girl all alone, just the two of them locked quietly away from prying eyes. True, it had turned out that a lot of his experiences had been judged by Venus and any other God who felt like looking in, but Forrester hadn't known that at the time and, in any case, the spectators had been invisible and thus ignorable.

Now, however, he was on the greensward of Central Park, within full view of a couple of thousand drunken revelers, all of whom, if not otherwise occupied, asked for nothing better than a good view of their God in action. And whichever girl he chose would leave six others eagerly awaiting their turns, watching his every move with appreciative eyes.

And on top of that, there was Gerda, close by. He was trying to keep an eye on her. But was she keeping an eye on him, too?

It didn't seem to matter much that she couldn't recognize him as William Forrester. She could still see him in action with the seven luscious maidens. The idea was appalling.

All afternoon, he had put off the inevitable by every method he could think of. He had danced with each of the girls in turn for entirely improbable lengths of time. He had performed high-jumps, leaps, barrel-rolls, Immelmann turns and other feats showing off his Godlike prowess to anyone interested. He had made a display of himself until he was sick of the whole business. He had consumed staggering amounts of ferment and distillate, and he had forced the stuff on the girls themselves, in the hope that, what with the liquor and the exertion, they would lie down on the grass and quietly pass out.

Unfortunately, none of these plans had worked. Dancing and acrobatics had to come to an end sometime, and as for the girls, what they wanted to do was lie down, not pass out-at least not from liquor.

The Chosen Maidens had been imbued, temporarily, with extraordinary staying powers by the Priests of the various temples, working with the delegated powers of the various Gods. After all, an ordinary girl couldn't be expected to keep up with Dionysus during a revel, could she? A God reveling was more than any ordinary mortal could take for long-as witness the ancient legend concerned the false Norse God, Thor.

But these girls were still raring to go, and the sun had set, and he was running out of opportunities for delay. He tried to think of some more excuses, and he couldn't think of one. Vaguely, he wished that the real Dionysus would show up. He would gladly give the God not only the credit, he told himself wearily, but the entire game.

He glanced out into the growing dimness. Gerda was out there still, with her brother and the oaf-whose name, Forrester had discovered, was Alvin Sherdlap. It was not a probable name, but Alvin did not look like a probable human being.

Now and again during the long afternoon, Forrester had got Ed Symes to toss up more rocks as targets, just to keep his hand in and to help him in keeping an eye on Gerda and her oaf, Alvin. It was a boring business, exploding rocks in mid-air, but after a while Symes apparently got to like it, and thought of it as a singular honor. After all, he had been picked for a unique position: target-tosser for the great God Dionysus. Who else could make that statement?

He would probably grow in the estimation of his friends, Forrester thought, and that was a picture that wouldn't stand much thinking about. As a stupefying boor, Symes was bad enough. Adding insufferable snobbishness to his present personality was piling Pelion on Ossa. And only a God, Forrester reminded himself wryly, could possibly do that.

Now, Forrester discovered, Symes and Alvin Sherdlap and Gerda were all sitting around a large keg of beer which Symes had somehow managed to appropriate from some other part of the grounds. He and Alvin were guzzling happily, and Gerda was just sitting there, whiling away the time, apparently, by thinking. Forrester wondered if she was thinking of him, and the notion made him feel sad and poetic.

Gerda couldn't see him any longer, he knew. The darkness of night had come down and there was no moon. The only illumination was the glow rising from the rest of the city, since the lights of the park would stay out throughout the night. To an ordinary mortal, the remaining light was not enough to see anything more than a few feet away. But to Forrester's Godlike, abnormally perceptive vision, the park seemed no darker than it had at dusk, an hour or so before. Though the Symes trio could not possibly see him, he could still watch over them with no effort at all.

He intended to continue doing so.

But now, with darkness putting a cloak over his activities, and his mind completely empty of excuses, was the time to begin the task at hand.

He cleared his throat and spoke very softly.

"Well," he said. "Well."

There had to be something to follow that, but for a minute he couldn't think of what.

Millicent giggled unexpectedly. "Oh, Lord Dionysus! I feel so *honored!*"

"Er," Forrester said. Finally he found words. "Oh, that's all right," he said, wondering exactly what he meant. "Perfectly all right, Millicent."

"Call me Millie."

"Of course, Millie."

"You can call me Bets, if you want to," Bette chimed in. Bette was a blonde with short, curly hair and a startling figure. "It's kind of a pet name. You know."

"Sure," Forrester said. "Uh-would you mind keeping your voices down a little?"

"Why?" Millicent asked.

Forrester passed a hand over his forehead. "Well," he said at last, thinking about Gerda, only a few feet away, "I thought it might be nicer if we were quiet. Sort of private and romantic."

"Oh," Bette said.

Kathy spoke up. "You mean we have to whisper? As if we were doing something secret?"

Forrester tightened his lips. He felt the beginnings of a strong distaste for Kathy. Why couldn't she leave well enough alone? But he only said: "Well, yes. I thought it might be fun. Let's try it, girls."

"Of course, Lord Dionysus," Kathy said demurely.

He disliked her, he decided, intensely.

There was a little silence.

"Well," Forrester said. "You're all such beautiful girls that I hardly know how to-ah-proceed from here."

Millicent tittered. So did one of the others-Judy, Forrester thought.

"I wouldn't want any of you to feel disappointed, or think you were any lower in my estimation than-than any other one of you." The sentence seemed to have got lost somewhere, Forrester thought, but he had straightened it out. "That wouldn't be fair," he went on, "and we Gods are always fair."

The sentence didn't ring quite true in Forrester's mind, and he thought he heard one of the girls snicker, but he ignored it and went bravely on.

"So," he said, "we're going to have a little game."

Millicent said: "Game?"

"Sure," Forrester said, trying his best to sound enthusiastic. "We all like games, don't we? I mean, what's an orgy—I mean, what's a revel-but a great big game? Isn't that right?"

"Well," Bette said doubtfully, "I guess so. Sure, Lord Dionysus, if you say so."

"Well, sure it is!" Forrester said. "Fun and games! So we'll play a little game. Ha-ha."

Kathy looked up at him brightly. "What kind of game, Lord Dionysus?" she asked in an innocent tone. She was an extravagantly pretty brunette with bright brown eyes, and she had been one of the two he had held in his arms during the Procession back from the uptown end of the park. Thinking it over now, Forrester wasn't entirely sure whether he had chosen her or she had chosen him, but it didn't really seem to matter, after all.

"Well, now," he said, "it's going to be a game of pure chance. Chance and nothing more."

"Like luck," Bette contributed.

"That's right-uh-Bets," Forrester said. "Like luck. And I promise not to use my powers to affect the outcome. Fair enough, isn't it?"

"Certainly," Kathy said demurely. There was really no reason for him to be irritated by the girl, so long as she was agreeing with him so nicely. Nevertheless, he wasn't quite sure that she was speaking her mind.

"Oh," Millicent said. "Sure."

Bette nodded. "Uh-huh. I mean, yes, Lord Dionysus."

Forrester waved a hand. "No need for formality," he said, and felt like an ass. But none of the girls seemed to notice. Agreement with his idea became general. "Well, let's see."

His eyes wandered over the surrounding scenery in quiet thought. Several Myrmidons were scattered about twenty feet away, and they were standing with their backs to the group as a matter of formality. If they had turned around, they couldn't have seen a thing in the darkness. But they had to remain at their stations, to make sure no unauthorized persons, souvenir-hunters, musicians, special-pleaders or just plain lost souls intruded upon great Dionysus while he was occupied.

The Myrmidons were the only living souls within that radius, except for Forrester himself and his bevy-and the Symes trio.

His gaze settled on them. Ed Symes, he noticed with quiet satisfaction, was now out cold. Forrester thought that the little spell he had cast on the beer might have had something to do with that, and he felt rather pleased with his efforts, at least in that direction. Symes was lying flat on his back, snoring loudly enough to drown out all but a few notes from the steam calliope, which was singing itself loudly to sleep somewhere in the distance. Near the prone figure, Gerda was trying to fend off the advances of good old Alvin Sherdlap, but it was obvious that the sheer passage of time, plus the amount of liquor she had consumed, were weakening her resistance.

Forrester pointed a finger at the man. The one thing he really wanted to do was to give Alvin the rock treatment. One little *zap* would do it, and Alvin Sherdlap would encumber the Earth no more. And it wasn't as if Alvin would be missed, Forrester told himself. It was clear from one look at the lout that no one, anywhere, for any reason, would miss Alvin if he were exploded into dust.

The temptation was very nearly irresistible, but somehow Forrester managed to resist it. He had been told that he had to be extremely careful in the use of his powers, and he had a pretty good idea that he wouldn't be able to justify blasting Alvin. Viewed objectively, there was nothing wrong with what the oaf was doing. He was merely following his religion as he understood it, and the religion was a very simple one: when at an orgy, have an orgy.

Gerda didn't have to give in if she didn't want to, Forrester thought. He tried very hard to make himself believe that.

But his finger was still pointed at the man. He didn't stop his powers entirely; he merely throttled them down so that only a tiny fraction of the neural energy at his command came into play. The energy that came from the tip of his finger made no noise and cast no light. It was not a killing blow.

Invisibly, it leaped across the intervening space and hit Alvin Sherdlap squarely on the nose.

The results were eminently satisfactory. Alvin uttered a sharp cry, let go of Gerda and fell over backward. His legs stood up straight in the air for a second, and then came down to hit the ground. He was silent. Gerda stared down at him, too tired and confused to make any coherent picture out of what was going on.

Forrester sighed happily to himself. *That*, he thought, *ought to take care of Alvin for a while.*

"Lord Dionysus," Kathy asked in that same innocent tone, "what are you pointing at out there?"

The girl was decidedly irritating, Forrester thought. "Pointing?" he said. "Ah, yes." He thought fast. "My target-tosser. I fear that his religious fervor has led to his being overcome."

The girls all turned round to look but, of course, Forrester thought, they could see nothing at all in the darkness.

"My goodness," Bette said.

"But if he's unconscious," Kathy put in, "why were you pointing at him?"

Forrester told himself that the next time the Sabbatical Bacchanal was held, he would see to it that an intelligence test was given to every candidate for Dionysian Escort, and anyone who scored as high on it as Kathy would be automatically disqualified.

He had to think of some excuse for looking at the man. And then he had it-the game he had planned. It was really quite a nice little idea.

"I hate to see the poor mortal miss out on the rest of the evening," Forrester said, "even if he is asleep now. And I think we may have a use for him."

He gestured gently with one hand.

Gerda and Alvin Sherdlap didn't even notice what was happening. They were much too busy arguing, Alvin claiming that somebody had slapped him on the nose —"and pretty hard, too, let me tell you!" —and Gerda swearing she hadn't done it. The fact that Ed Symes's snores were fading quietly into the distance dawned on neither of them.

But Ed was in flight. He rose five feet above the ground, still unconscious and snoring, and sped unerringly across the air, like a large, fat arrow shot from a bow, in the direction of Forrester and the circle of girls.

He appeared overhead suddenly, and Forrester controlled him so that he drifted downward as delicately as an overweight snowflake, eddying in the slight breeze while the girls gaped at him. Forrester allowed the body to drop the last six inches out of control, so that Ed Symes landed with a heavy thump in the center of the circle. But no harm was done. Ed was very far gone indeed; he merely snored on.

"There," Forrester said.

Millicent blinked. "Where?" she said. "Him?"

"Certainly," Forrester said in a pleased tone. "He's a good deal too noisy, though, don't you think?"

"He snores a lot," Judy offered in a tentative voice, "if that's what you mean, Lord Dionysus."

"Exactly. And I don't see any reason to put up with it. Instead, well just put him in stasis for a little while, and that'll keep him quiet." Again he waved one hand, almost carelessly. Ed Symes's snores vanished immediately, leaving the world a cleaner, purer, quieter place to live in, and his body became as rigid as if he were a statue.

"There," Forrester said again with satisfaction.

"Now what?" Kathy asked.

"Now we straighten him out."

One more pass, and Ed Symes's arms were at his sides, his legs stretched straight out. Only his stomach projected above the rigid lines of his body. Forrester thought he had never seen a more pleasing sight.

Dorothy gasped. "Is he-is he dead?"

Forrester looked at her reprovingly. "Dead? Now what would I do that for, after he's been so helpful and all?"

"I don't know," she muttered.

"Well," Forrester said, "he's not dead. He's just in stasis-in a state of totally suspended animation. As soon as I take the spell off, he'll be all right. But I don't think I'll take it off just yet. I've got plans for my little target-tosser."

He reached over and touched the stiff body. It seemed to rise a fraction of an inch, floating on the tips of the grass. The wind stirred it a little, but it didn't float away.

"I took some of his weight off," Forrester explained, "so he'll be a little easier to handle."

Now Ed Symes was behaving as if he were a statue carved out of cork. With a quick flip, Forrester turned the statue over. The effect was exactly what he wanted. Ed did not touch the grass at any point except one: the point where his protuberant stomach most protruded. Fore and aft, the rest of him was balanced stiffly in the air.

Forrester gazed at the sight, feeling fulfilled. "Now," he said with a note of decision in his voice, "we are going to play Spin-the-Bottle!"

The girls giggled and laughed.

"You mean with him?" Bette said.

Forrester sighed. "That's right," he said patiently. "With him."

He got into position and looked up at the girls. "This one's just for practice, so we can all see how it works." He gave Symes's extended foot a little push.

Whee! he thought. Round and round the gentleman went, spinning quietly on his stomach, revolving in a merry fashion while the girls and Forrester watched silently. At last he slowed and stopped, his nose pointing at Bette and his toes at Dorothy.

"Oh, my!" Dorothy said. "He's pointing at me!"

"He is not!" Bette said decisively. "His head points my way!"

"But he —"

"Temper, temper," Forrester said. "No arguments. That one didn't count, anyhow-it was just to see how he worked. And I do think he works very nicely, don't you?"

"Oh, yes, Lord Dionysus," Kathy said. There was the same undertone in her voice, as if she were silently laughing at everything. She was, he told himself, an extremely unlikable young woman.

The other girls agreed in a chorus. They were still studying the stiff body of Ed Symes. His stomach had made a little depression in the grass as he whirled, and he was now nicely bedded down for a real spin. Forrester rubbed his hands together.

"Fine," he said. "Now, all of you are going to be judges."

"Me, too?" Bette asked.

Forrester nodded. "The head will be the determining factor. If our little Mr. Bottle's head points to any one of you, that is the one I'll choose first."

"See?" Bette said. "I told you it was his head."

"Well, I couldn't tell before anybody said so," Dorothy said. "And anyhow, I —"

"Now, now, girls," Forrester said, feeling momentarily like a Girl Scout troop leader. "Let's listen to the rules, shall we? And then we can get down to playing the game." He took a deep breath. "Isn't this fun?"

The girls giggled.

"Good," Forrester said. "If Mr. Bottle's head ends up between two of you, then the other five girls will have to decide which girl the head's nearer to. The two girls involved will remain absolutely quiet during the judging, and if the other five can't come to a unanimous agreement, we'll spin Mr. Bottle again. Understand?"

"You mean if the head points at me, I get picked," Bette said. "And if the head goes in between me and somebody else, all the other girls have to decide who gets picked."

It was a masterly summation.

"Right," Forrester said. "I'm going to give Mr. Bottle a spin. This one counts. We'll have the second spin, and the rest of them, later."

"Gee!" Millicent whispered. "Isn't this *exciting*?"

Forrester ignored the comment. "And remember, I give you my word as a God that I will not interfere in any way with the workings of chance. Is that clearly understood?"

The girls murmured agreement.

"Now," Forrester said, "all you girls get into a nice circle. I'll stand outside."

The girls took a minute or two arranging themselves in a circle, arguing about who was going to sit next to whom, and whose very proximity was bound to bring bad luck. The argument gave Forrester a chance to check on Gerda again. She was whispering softly to Alvin, but they weren't touching each other. Forrester turned up his hearing to get a better idea of what was going on.

They had progressed, in the usual manner, from argument to life-history. Gerda was telling Alvin all about her past.

"...but don't misunderstand me, Alvin. It's just that I was in love with a very fine young man. An Athenan, he was. A wonderful man, really wonderful. But he-he was killed in a subway accident some months ago."

"Gosh," Alvin said. "I'm sorry."

"I—I have to tell you this, Alvin, so you'll understand. I still love him. He was wonderful. And until I get over it, I simply can't..."

Feeling both ashamed of himself and pleased, as well as sorry for the poor girl, Forrester quit listening. The Gods had arranged his simulated death, which, of course, had been a necessity. His disappearance had to be explained somehow. But he didn't like the idea of Gerda having to suffer so much.

My God! Forrester thought. *She still loves me!*

It was the first time he had ever heard her say so, flatly, right out in the open. He wanted to bound and leap and cavort-but he couldn't. He had to go back to his seven beautiful girls.

He had never felt less like it in his life.

But at least, he consoled himself, Gerda was keeping Alvin at arm's length. She was being faithful to his memory.

Faithful-because she loved him.

Grimly, he turned back to the girls. "Well, are we all ready now?"

Kathy looked up at him brightly. "Lord Dionysus, it's so dark I can't even see for sure what's going on. How can we do any judging, if we can't see?"

Forrester cursed Kathy for pointing out the flaw in his arrangements. Then, making a nice impartial job of it, he cursed himself for forgetting that what was perfectly visible to him was dark night to mortals.

"We can clear that up," he said quickly. "As a matter of fact, I was just getting around to it. We will now proceed to shed a little light on the subject-said subject being our old friend Mr. Bottle."

The trick had been taught to him by Venus, but he'd never had a chance to practice it. This was his first real experience with it, and he could only hope that it went off as it was supposed to.

He stepped into the middle of the circle, near Ed Symes's stiff body and held his right hand above his head, thumb and forefinger spread an inch apart and the other three fingers folded into his palm.

Then he concentrated.

A long second ticked by, while Forrester tried to apply even more neural pressure. Then...

A small ball of light appeared between his thumb and forefinger, a yellow, cold sphere of fire that shed its radiance over the whole group. Carefully, he withdrew his hand, not daring to breathe. The ball of yellow fire remained in position, hanging in mid-air.

The muffled gasp from the circle of girls was, Forrester told himself, a definite tribute.

"Now don't worry about it, girls," he said. "That light's only visible to the eight of us. Nobody else can see it."

There was another little series of gasps.

Forrester grinned. "Can everybody see each other?"

A murmur of agreement.

"Can everybody see Mr. Bottle here?"

Another murmur.

"In that case, let's go." He stepped outside the circle of girls, reached in again for Ed Symes's foot, and set the gentleman spinning once more.

Symes spun with a blinding speed, making a low, whistling noise. Forrester watched the body spin dizzily, just as anxious as the girls were to find out who the first winner was going to be. He thought of Millicent, who chewed gum and made it pop. He thought of Bette, the inveterate explainer and double-take expert. He tried to think of Dorothy and Jayne and Beverly and Judy, but the thought of Kathy, irritating and uncomfortable and too damned bright for her own good, got annoyingly in the way.

He was rather glad he had promised not to use his powers on the spinning figure. He was not at all sure which one of the girls he would have picked for Number One.

And he had, after all, given his word as a God. True, he wasn't quite a God, only a demi-Deity. But he did feel that Dionysus might object to his name being used in vain. A promise, he told himself sternly and with some relief, was a promise.

After some time, Mr. Ed (Bottle) Symes began to slow perceptibly. The whistling died as Symes began rotating about his abdominal axis at a more and more leisurely rate. Seconds passed. Symes faced Bette ... Millicent ... Kathy ... Judy ... Bette again...

Forrester watched, fascinated.

Finally, Symes came to a halt. All the elaborate instructions in case the Bottle ended up pointing between two girls had been, Forrester saw, totally unnecessary. Symes's head was pointing at one girl, and one girl alone.

She gave a little squeal of delight. The others began chorusing their congratulations at once, looking no more convincing than the runners-up in any beauty contest. Their smiles appeared to have been glued on loosely, and their voices lacked a certain something. Possibly it was sincerity.

"All right, that's it for now." Forrester turned to the winner. "My congratulations," he said, wondering just what he was supposed to say. Not finding any appropriate words, he turned back to the group of six losers. "The rest of you girls can do me a big favor. Go get a couple of the Myrmidons to protect you, hunt around for the nearest wine barrel and confiscate it for me. It's been a thirsty day."

"Gee," Jayne said. "Sure we will, Lord Dionysus."

"Now take your time," Forrester said, and the losers all giggled at once, like a trained chorus. Forrester grimaced. "Don't come back till you find a barrel. Then we'll play the game again."

In a disappointed fashion, the six of them trooped off into the darkness and vanished to mortal eyes. Forrester watched them go and then turned to the winner, feeling just a little uncertain.

"Well, Kathy," he started. "I —"

She flung herself on him with the avid girlishness of a Bengal tiger. "I have dreamed of this night since I was but a child! At last I am in your arms! I love you! Take me! I am yours, all yours!"

"That's nice," Forrester said, taken far aback by the girl's sudden onslaught. His immediate impulse was to unwind Kathy and set her back on her own feet, some little distance away, after which he could start again on a more leisurely basis. After all, he told himself, people ought to spend more time getting to know each other.

But he remembered, just in time, that he was Dionysus. He conquered his first impulse and put his arms around her. As he did so, he discovered that his face was being covered with kisses. Kathy was murmuring little indistinct terms of endearment into his ear every time she reached it en route from one side of his face to the other.

Forrester swallowed hard, tightened his grip and planted his lips firmly on Kathy's. A blaze of startling heat shot through him.

In a small corner at the back of his mind, a scroll unrolled. On it was written what Vulcan had told him about his mental attitude changing after Investiture. When he had been plain William Forrester, an attack like the one Kathy was making on him had pretty much chilled him for a while. But now he found himself definitely rising to the occasion.

There was a passion to her kiss that he had never felt before, a rising tide of flame that threatened to char him. The movement of her mouth on his sent new fires burning throughout his body, and as her hands moved on him he was awakened to a new world, a world of consuming desires.

He wished his own clothing away, and fumbled for a second at the two fastenings that held Kathy's *chiton* in place. Then it was gone and there was nothing between them. They met, flesh to flesh, in a fiery embrace that grew as he forced her down and she responded eagerly, wildly, to his every motion. His lips traveled over her; her entire body was drowning him once and for all in an unbelievable red haze, unlike anything he had ever before experienced ... a great wave of passion that went on and on, rising to a peak he had never dreamed of until his body shivered with the sensations, and he pressed on, rising still higher in an ecstasy beyond measure....

His last spasm of tension turned out the God-light.

She lay in his arms on the grass, holding him almost as tightly as he held her. He felt exhausted, but he knew perfectly well that he wasn't. A God was a God, after all, and Kathy was only the hors d'oeuvres of a seven-course dinner.

"You're wonderful," Kathy said in a soft whisper at his ear. "Absolutely wonderful. More wonderful than I could ever dream. I —"

She was interrupted by a strange, harsh voice that bellowed from somewhere nearby.

"All right, bitch!" it said. "Get the hell up from there! And you too, buster!"

Forrester jerked his head up in astonishment and froze. Kathy looked up, fright written all over her face.

The man standing over them in the darkness looked like a prize-fighter, one who had taken a number of beatings, but always given better than he had received. His arms were akimbo, his feet planted as firmly as if he were a particularly stubborn brand of tree. He glared down at them, his face expressive of anger, hatred-and, Forrester thought dully, a complete lack of respect for his God.

The man barked: "You heard what I said! On your feet, buster! If I have to kick your teeth in, I want to do it when you're standing up!"

Forrester's jaw dropped. Then, as the initial shock left him, anger boiled in to take its place. He toyed with the idea of blasting this mortal who showed such disrespect to a God. He sprang to his feet, ready to move, and then stopped.

Maybe the man was crazy. Maybe he was just some poor soul who wasn't responsible for his own actions. It would be merciful, Forrester thought, to find out first, and blast the intruder afterward.

He looked around. Twenty yards away, the encircling Myrmidons still stood, their backs to the scene, as if nothing at all were going on.

Forrester blinked. "How'd you get in here, anyway?"

The man barked a laugh. "None of your business." He turned to Kathy, who had devoted the previous few seconds to getting her *chiton* on again. Hurriedly, Forrester wished back his own costume. Kathy got up, staring straight back at the intruder. Fear was gone from her face, and a kind of calmness that Forrester had never seen before possessed her now.

"So!" the intruder bellowed. "The minute my back is turned, off you go! By the Stars and Galaxy, I —I don't know what to call you! You're worse than your predecessor! Can't turn anything down! You —"

"Now wait!" Forrester bellowed in his most Godlike voice. "Just hold still there! Do you know who you're talking to? How dare you —"

And Kathy interrupted him. Forrester stood mute as she stripped the stranger with a voice like scalding acid. "Listen, you," she said, pointing a finger at the man. "Who do you think you are-my husband?"

"By the Stars —" the stranger began.

"Don't bother trying to scare me with your big mouth," Kathy went on imperturbably. "You don't mean a thing to me and you can't order me around. What's more, you know it. You're not my husband, you big thug-and you're never going to be. I'll sleep with whomever I please, and whenever I please, and wherever I please, and that's the way things are going to be. After all, lard-head, it's my job, isn't it? Got any questions?"

Her *job*?

Forrester began to wonder just what he had managed to walk into now. But that was a detail. The important thing was that his Godhood had been grossly, unbelievably insulted-and at a damned inconvenient time, too!

He stepped between Kathy and the intruder, his eyes flashing fire. "Do you know who I am? Do you know that —"

"Of course he knows," Kathy put in abruptly. "And if you don't want to get hurt, I'd advise you to stay out of this little quarrel."

Forrester turned and stared at her.

What the everlasting bloody hell was going *on*?

But there wasn't any time to think. The intruder put his face up near Forrester's and glared at him. "Sure I know who you are, buster," he said. "You're a wise guy. You're a Johnny-come-lately. And I know what I ought to do with you, too-take you apart, limb by limb!"

That did it. Forrester, seeing several shades of red, decided that no God could possibly object if this ugly blasphemer were blasted off the face of the Earth. He raised a hand.

And Kathy grabbed it. *"Don't!"* she said in a frightened tone.

The intruder grinned wolfishly at him. "Pay no attention to Little Miss Sacktime over there, Forrester. You go right ahead and try it! All I need is an excuse to vaporize you. Just one tiny little excuse-and I'll do the job so damn quick, your head won't even have time to start swimming." He set himself. "Go on. Let's see your stuff, Forrester."

Forrester's arm came down, without his being aware of it. There was only room in his mind for one thought.

The intruder had called him Forrester.

Where had he gotten the name?

And, for that matter, how had he seen the two of them in the darkness?

While the questions were still spinning in Forrester's mind, Kathy threw herself forward between him and the stranger. "Ares!" she screamed. "You stupid, jealous idiot! Get some sense into that battle-scarred brain of yours! Are you completely crazy?"

"Now you listen to me —" the stranger began.

"Listen, nothing! If you want to pick a fight, do it with me —I can fight back! But if you lay a hand on Forrester, we'll never find another —"

The stranger reached out casually and clamped one huge paw over her mouth. "Shut up," he said, almost quietly. He glanced at Forrester and went on, in the same tone: "Don't give away everything you've got, chum."

A second passed and then he took the hand away. Kathy said nothing at all for a moment, and then she nodded.

"All right," she said. "You're right. We shouldn't be losing our tempers just now. But I didn't start —"

"Didn't you?" the stranger said.

Kathy shrugged. "Well, never mind it now." She turned to Forrester. "You know who we are now, don't you?"

Forrester nodded very slowly. How else could the man have come through the cordon of Myrmidons and seen them in the darkness? How else would he have dared to face up to Dionysus-confident that he could beat him? And how else could all this argument have gone on without anyone hearing it?

For that matter, why else would the argument have begun-unless the stranger and Kathy were —

"Sure," he said, as if he had known it all along. "You're Mars and Venus."

He could feel cold death approaching.

CHAPTER 10

William Forrester sat, quite alone, in the room which had been given him on Mount Olympus. He stared out of the window, a little smaller than the window in Venus' rooms, at the Grecian plain far below, without actually seeing. There was no vertigo this time; small matters like that couldn't bother him.

The whole room was rather a small one, as Gods' rooms went, but it had the same varicolored shifting walls, the same furniture that appeared when you approached it. Forrester was beginning to get used to it now, and he didn't know if it was going to do him any good.

He peered down, trying to discern the patrolling Myrmidons around the base and lower slopes of the mountain, placed there to discourage overeager climbers from trying to reach the home of the Gods. Of course he couldn't see them, and after a while he lost interest again. Matters were too serious to allow time for that kind of game.

The Autumn Bacchanal was over, a thing of the past, on the way to the distortion of legend. Forrester's greatest triumph had ended-in his greatest fiasco.

He closed his eyes as he sat in his room, the fluctuating colors on the walls going unappreciated. He had nothing to do now except wait for the final judgment of the Gods.

At first he had been terrified. But terror could only last so long, and, as the time ticked by, the idea of that coming judgment had almost stopped troubling his mind. Either he had passed the tests or he hadn't. There was no point in worrying about the inevitable. He felt anesthetized, numb to any sensation of personal danger. There was nothing whatever he could do. The Gods had him; very well, let the Gods worry about what to do with him.

Freed, his mind turned over and over a problem that seemed new to him at first. Gradually, he realized it wasn't new at all; it had been somewhere in the back of his thoughts from the very first, when Venus had told him that he had been chosen as a double for Dionysus, so many months ago. It seemed like years to Forrester, and yet, at the same time, like no more than hours. So much had happened, and so much had changed....

But the question had remained, waiting until he could look at it and work with it. Now he could face that strange doubt in his mind, the doubt that had colored everything since his introduction to the Gods, that had grown as his training in demi-Godhood had progressed, and that was now, for the first time, coming to full consciousness. Every time it had come near the surface, before this day, he had expelled it from his mind, forcefully getting rid of it without realizing fully that he was doing so.

And perhaps, he thought, the doubt had begun even earlier than that. Perhaps he had always doubted, and never allowed himself to think about the doubt. The floor of his mind seemed to open and he was falling, falling....

But where the doubt had begun was unimportant now. It was present, it had grown; that was all that mattered. He could find facts to feed the doubt and strengthen it, and he looked at the facts one by one:

First there was the angry conversation between Mars and Venus, on the night of the Bacchanal.

He could still hear what Mars had said:

"... *worse than your predecessor*."

And then he'd shut Venus up before she gave away too much-realizing, maybe, that he had given away a good deal himself. That one little sentence was enough to bring everything into question, Forrester thought.

He had wondered why it had been necessary to have a double for Dionysus, but he hadn't actually thought about it; maybe he hadn't wanted to think about it. But now, with the notion of a "predecessor" for Venus in his mind, he *had* to think about it, and the only conclusion he could come to was a disturbing one. It did more than disturb him, as a matter of fact-it frightened him. He wanted desperately to find some flaw in the conclusion he faced, because he feared it even more than he feared the coming judgment of the Pantheon.

But there wasn't any flaw. The facts meshed together entirely too well to be an accidental pattern.

In the first place, he thought, why had he been picked for the job? He was a nobody, of no importance, with no special gifts. Why did he deserve the honor of taking his place beside Hercules and Achilles and Odysseus and the other great heroes? Forrester knew he wasn't any hero. But what gave him his standing?

And, he went on, there was a second place. In the months of his training he had met fourteen of the Gods-all of them, except for Dionysus. Now, what kind of sense did that make? Anyone who's going to have a double usually trains the double himself, if it's at all possible. Or, at the very least, he allows the double to watch his actions, so that the double can do a really competent job of imitation.

And if an imitation is all that's needed, why not hire an actor instead of a history professor?

Vulcan had told him: "You were picked not merely for your physical resemblance to Dionysus, but your psychological resemblance as well."

That had to be true, if only because, as far as Forrester could see, nobody had the slightest reason to lie about it. But why should it be true? What advantage did the Gods get out of that "psychological resemblance"? All he was supposed to be was a double-and anybody who *looked* like Dionysus would be accepted *as* Dionysus by the people. The "psychological resemblance" didn't have a single thing to do with it.

Mars, Venus, Vulcan-even Zeus had dropped clues. Zeus had referred to him as a "substitute for Dionysus."

A substitute, he realized with a kind of horror, was not at all the same thing as a double.

The answer was perfectly clear, but there were even more facts to bolster it. Why had he been tested, for instance, *after* he had been made a demi-God? In spite of what Vulcan had said, was he slated for further honors if he passed the new tests? He was sure that Vulcan had been telling the truth as far as he'd gone-but it hadn't been the whole truth. Forrester was certain of that now.

And what was it that Venus had said during that argument with Mars? Something about not killing Forrester, because then they would have to "get another —"

Another *what*?

Another *substitute*?

No, there was no escape from the simple and obvious conclusion. Dionysus was either missing, which was bad enough, or something much worse.

He was dead.

Forrester shivered. The idea of an immortal God dying was, in one way, as horrible a notion as he could imagine. But in another way, it seemed to make a good deal of sense. As far as plain William Forrester had been concerned, the contradiction in the notion of a dead immortal would have made it ridiculous to start with. But the demi-God Dionysus had a somewhat different slant on things.

After all, as Vulcan had told him, a demi-God could die. And if that was true, then why couldn't a God die too? Perhaps it would take quite a lot to kill a God-but the difference would be one of degree, not of kind.

It seemed wholly logical. And it led, Forrester saw, to a new conclusion, one that required a little less effort to face than he thought it would. It should have shaken the foundations of his childhood and left him dizzy, but somehow it didn't. How long, he asked himself, had he been secretly doubting the fact that the Gods were Gods?

At least in the sense they pretended to be, the "Gods" were not gods at all. They were-something else.

But what? Where did they come from?

Were they actually the Gods of ancient Greece, as they claimed? Forrester wanted to throw that claim out with the rest, but when he thought things over he didn't see why he should. To an almost indestructible being, three thousand years may only be a long time.

So the Gods actually were "Gods," at least as far as longevity went. But the decision didn't get him very far; there were still a lot of questions unanswered, and no way that he could see of answering them.

Or, rather, there was one way, but it was hellishly dangerous. He had no business even thinking about. He was in enough hot water already.

Nevertheless....

What more harm could he do to his chances? After the Bacchanal fiasco, there was probably a sentence of death hanging over his head anyhow. And they couldn't do any more to him than kill him.

It was ridiculous, he told himself, with a return of caution and sanity. But the notion came back, nagging at his mind, and at last it took a new form.

The Gods had the rest of the information he needed. He had to go to one of them-but which one?

His first thought was Venus. But, after a moment of thought, he ruled her regretfully out as a possibility. After all, there was Mars' mention of her "predecessor." If that meant anything, it meant that the current Venus wasn't the original one. She would have a lot less information than one of the original Gods.

If there were any originals left....

He tabled that thought hurriedly and went on. Vulcan had told him at least a part of the truth, and Vulcan looked like a good bet. Forrester didn't like the idea of bearding the artisan in his workshop; it made him feel uncomfortable, and after a while he put his finger on the reason. His little liaison with Venus made him feel guilty. There was, he knew, no real reason for it. In the first place, he hadn't known the girl was Venus, and in the second place she may not have been the same one who had been Vulcan's original wife, thirty and more centuries ago.

But the guilt remained, and he tabled Vulcan for the time being and went on.

Morpheus, Hera, and most of the others he passed by without a glance; there was no reason for them to dislike him, but there was no reason for comradeship, either. Mars popped into his mind, and popped right out again. That would be putting his head in the lion's mouth with a vengeance.

No, there was only one left, the obvious choice, the one who had helped him throughout his training period-Diana. She genuinely seemed to like him. She was also a good kid. The thought alone was almost enough to make him smile fondly, and would have if he had not remembered the peril he was in.

He turned away from the window to look at the color-swirled wall across the room. He had remained in his room ever since Mars and Venus had brought him back from New York, and he wasn't at all sure that he could leave it. In the normal sense of the word, the place had neither exits nor entrances. The only way of getting in or out of the place was via the Veils of Heaven-matter transmitters, not something supernatural, he realized now.

As far as Forrester knew, they still worked. But the Gods could generate a Veil anywhere, at any time. Forrester, as a demi-God, could only will one into existence on sufferance; he could only work the matter-transmitting Veils if the Gods permitted him to do so. If they didn't, he was trapped.

Well, he told himself, there was one way to find out.

He walked over to the wall and stood a few feet away from it, concentrating in the way he had been taught. He was still slower at it than the Gods themselves, and hadn't developed the knack of forming a Veil as he walked toward the place where he wanted it to be, as they had.

But he knew he could do it-if he was still allowed to.

Minutes went by.

Then, as the blue sheet of neural energy flickered into being, Forrester slumped in sudden relief. He took a deep breath and closed his eyes.

The Veil was there-but was it what he hoped, or a trick? Possibly he could focus the other terminal where he wanted it, but there was also the chance that the Gods had set the thing up so that, when he stepped through, he would be standing in the Court of the Gods facing a tribunal for which he was totally unprepared.

It would be just like the Pantheon, he thought, to pull a lousy trick like that.

But there was no point in dithering. If death was to be his fate, that would be that. He could do nothing at all by sitting in his room and waiting for them to come and get him.

He focused the exit terminal in Diana's apartment. There was no way of knowing whether the focus worked or not until he stepped through.

He opened his eyes and walked into the Veil.

He felt almost disappointed when he looked around him. He had steeled himself to do great battle with the Gods-and, instead, he was where he had wanted to be, in Diana's apartment.

She was standing with her back to him, and Forrester didn't make a sound, not wanting to startle the Goddess. She was totally unclad, her glorious body shining in the light of the room, her blue-black hair unbound and falling halfway down her gently curved back. But she must have heard him somehow, for she turned, and for half a second she stood facing him.

Forrester did not move. He couldn't even breathe.

Every magnificent curve was highlighted in a frozen tableau.

Then there was a sudden flash of white, and she was clad in a clinging *chiton* which, Forrester saw, served only to remind one of what one had recently seen. It worked very well, although Forrester did not think he had any need for an aid to his memory.

"My goodness!" Diana said. "You shouldn't surprise a girl like that! I mean, you really gave me a shock, kid!"

Forrester took his first breath. "Well," he said, "I could be dishonest, not to mention un-gallant, and tell you I was sorry."

"But?" Diana said.

"Being of sound mind and sound body, I'm a long way from being sorry."

And Diana dropped her eyes and blushed.

Forrester could barely believe it.

But it did show a part of the Goddess's personality that was entirely new to him. He was sure that any of the Gods or Goddesses could sense when a Veil of Heaven was forming near them, and get prepared before it was well enough developed to allow for passage. But Diana-who was, after all, one of the traditionally virgin Goddesses, like Pallas Athena-had chosen to pretend surprise.

Forrester had a further hunch, too. He thought she might have deliberately vanished her *chiton* only a second or so before he entered. And that put a different-and a very interesting-face on things.

Not to mention, he thought, an entire figure.

But he didn't say anything. That wasn't his main business in Diana's apartment. Instead, he watched her smile briskly and say: "Well, you're here, anyhow, kid, and I guess that's enough for me. Want a drink? I could whip up some nectar-and maybe an ambrosia sandwich?"

"I'll take the drink," Forrester said. "I'm not really hungry, thanks."

Diana held out her hands, fingers curved inward, and a crystal cup of clear, golden liquid appeared in each-matter transmission, of course, not magic. She handed one over to Forrester, who took it and looked the Goddess straight in the eyes.

"Thanks," he said. "Diana, I've got some questions to ask you, and I hope I'll get the answers."

She touched the rim of her cup to his. Her voice was very soft, but she didn't hesitate in the least. "I'll answer any questions I have to. Sit down."

They found chairs along the walls of the room and sat facing one another. Forrester took a sip of his drink, settled back, and tried to think where to begin. Well, God or no God, Zeus had the key to that one. He had said it years ago, and it had passed almost into legend:

"Begin at the beginning, go on until you reach the end, and then stop."

Very well, Forrester thought. He cleared his throat. Diana looked at him inquiringly.

"I don't know how far into the noose I'm putting my head with this one, Diana," he said. "But I trust you-and I've got to ask somebody."

"Go ahead," she said quietly.

"First question. The original Dionysus is dead, isn't he?"

She paused for a moment before answering. "Yes, he is."

"And I was scheduled to take his place."

"That's right."

"As a full God," Forrester said.

Diana nodded.

There was a little silence.

"Diana," Forrester said, "what are the Gods?"

She got up and crossed to the window. Looking out, she said: "Before I answer that, I want you to tell me what you think we are."

"Men and women," he said. "More or less human, like myself. Except you've somehow managed to get so far ahead of any kind of science Earth knows that, even today, your effects can only be explained as 'magic' or 'miracle.'"

"How could we get that far ahead of you?"

Forrester took a leap in the dark to the only conclusion he could see. "You're not from Earth," he said. "You're from another planet." The words sounded strange in his own ears-but Diana didn't even act surprised.

"That's right," she said. "We're from another planet-or, rather, from several other planets."

"*Several?*" Forrester exclaimed. "But-oh. I see. Pan, for instance —"

Diana nodded. "Pan isn't even really humanoid. His home is a planet where his type of goatlike life evolved. Neither Pluto nor Neptune is humanoid, either; they're a little closer than Pan, but not really very close when you get a good look. The rest of the Gods are humanoid-but not human."

"Wait a minute," Forrester said. "Venus is human. Or, anyhow, she's a replacement, just the way I was slated to be a replacement for Dionysus."

Diana drained her cup and clapped her hands together on it. The cup vanished. Forrester did the same to his own. "Correct," she said. "Venus just-just disappeared once. They got an Etruscan girl to replace her. She's not the only replacement, either."

Forrester stared. "Who else?"

"You tell me."

He thought the list of Gods over. "Zeus," he said.

Diana smiled. "Yes, Zeus is a long way from the great hero of the legends, isn't he? Using the old calendar, Zeus died in about 1100 b.c., not too long after the close of the Trojan War. As far as anybody knows, Neptune did the actual killing, but it's pretty clear that the original idea wasn't his."

"Hera's," Forrester guessed.

"Of course," Diana said. "What she wanted was a figurehead she could control-and that's what she got. Though I'm not sure she's entirely happy with the change. If the original Zeus was a little harder to control, at least he seems to have had an original thought now and again."

Forrester sat quietly for a time, waiting for the shock to pass. "What about Dionysus?"

Diana shrugged. "He-well, as far as anybody's ever been able to tell, it was suicide. About three years ago, and it drove Hera pretty wild, trying to find a substitute in a hurry. I suspect he was bored with the wine, women and song. He'd had a long time of it. And, too, he'd had some little disagreements with Hera. As you may have gathered, she is not exactly a safe person to have as an enemy. He probably figured she'd get him sooner or later, so he might as well save her the trouble."

"And Hera had to rush to get a replacement? Why couldn't there just have been some sort of explanation, while the rest of you ran things?"

"Because the rest of us couldn't run things. Not for long, anyhow. It's all a question of power."

"Power?" Forrester said.

"Everything we have," Diana said, "is derived, directly or indirectly, from the workings of one machine. Though 'machine' is a long way from the right word for it-it bears about as much resemblance to what you think of as a machine as a television set does to a window. There just isn't a word for it in any language you know."

"And all the Gods have to work the machine at once?"

"Something like that." Diana came back from the window and sat down facing him again. "It operates through the nervous systems of the beings in circuit with it, each one of them in contact with one of the power nodes of the machine. And if one of the nodes is unoccupied, then the machine's out of balance. It will run for a while, but eventually it will simply wreck itself. Every one of the fifteen nodes has to be occupied. Otherwise-chaos."

Forrester nodded. "So when Dionysus died —"

"We had to find a replacement in a hurry. The machine's been running out of balance for about as long as it can stand right now."

Forrester closed his eyes. "I'm not sure I get the picture."

"Well, look at it this way: suppose you have a wheel."

"All right," Forrester said obligingly. "I have a wheel."

"And this wheel has fifteen weights on it. They're spaced equally around the rim, and the wheel's revolving at high speed."

Forrester kept his eyes closed. When he had the wheel nicely spinning, he said: "Okay. Now what?"

"Well," Diana said, "as long as the weights stay in place, the wheel spins evenly. But if you remove one of the weights, the wheel's out of balance. It starts to wobble."

Forrester took one of the weights (Dionysus, a rather large, jolly weight) off the wheel in his mind. It wobbled. "Right," he said.

"It can take the wobble for a little while. But unless the balance is restored in time, the wheel will eventually break."

Hurriedly, Forrester put Dionysus back on the wheel. The wobble stopped. "Oh," he said. "I see."

"Our power machine works in that sort of way. That is, it requires all fifteen occupants. Dionysus has been dead for three years now, and that's about the outside limit. Unless he's replaced soon, the machine will be ruined."

Forrester opened his eyes. The wheel spun away and disappeared. "So you found me to replace Dionysus. I had to look like him, so the mortals wouldn't see any difference. And the psychological similarity —"

"That's right," Diana said. "It's the same as the wheel again. If you remove a weight, you've got to put back a weight of the same magnitude. Otherwise, the wheel's still out of balance."

"And since the power machine works through the nervous system —"

"The governing factor is that similarity. You've got to be of the same magnitude as Dionysus. Of course, you don't have to be an *identical* copy. The machine can be adjusted for *slight* differences."

"I see," Forrester said. "And the fifteen power nodes —" Another idea occurred to him. "Wait a minute. If there are only fifteen power nodes, then how come there were so many different Gods and Goddesses among the Greeks? There were a lot more than fifteen back then."

"Of course there were," Diana said, "but they weren't real Gods. As a matter of fact, some of them didn't really exist."

Forrester frowned. "How's that again?"

"They were just disguises for one of the regular fifteen. Aesculapius, for instance, the old God of medicine, was Hermes/Mercury in disguise-he took the name in honor of a physician of the time. He would have raised the man to demi-Godhood, but Aesculapius died unexpectedly, and we thought taking his 'spirit' into the Pantheon was good public relations."

"How about the others?" Forrester said. "They weren't all disguises, were they?"

"Of course not. Some of them were demi-Gods, just like yourself. Their power was derived, like yours, from the Pantheon instead of directly through the machine. And then there were the satyrs and centaurs, and suchlike beings. That was public relations, too-mainly Zeus' idea, I understand. The original Zeus, of course."

"Of course," Forrester said.

"The satyrs and such were artificial life-forms, created, maintained and controlled by the machine itself. It's equipped with what you might call a cybernetic brain-although that's pretty inadequate as a description. Vulcan could do a better job of explaining."

"Perfectly all right. I don't understand that kind of thing anyhow."

"Well, in that case, let me put it this way. The machine controlled these artificial forms, but they could be taken over by any one of the Gods or demi-Gods for special purposes. As I say, it was public relations-and a good way to keep the populace impressed-and under control."

"The creatures aren't around nowadays," Forrester pointed out.

"Nowadays we don't need them," Diana said. "There are other methods-better public relations, I suppose."

Forrester didn't know he was going to ask his next question until he heard himself doing so. But it was the question he really wanted to ask; he knew that as soon as he knew he asked it.

"Why?" he said.

Diana looked at him with a puzzled expression. "Why? What do you mean?"

"Why go on being Gods? Why dominate humanity?"

"I suppose I could answer your question with another question-why not? But I won't. Instead, let me remind you of some things. Look what we've done during the last century. The great wars that wrecked Europe-you don't see any possibility of more of those, do you? And the threat of atomic war is gone, too, isn't it?"

"Well, yes," Forrester said, "but —"

"But we still have wars," Diana said. "Sure we do. The male animal just wouldn't be happy if he didn't have a chance to go out and get himself blown to bits once in a while. Don't ask *me* to explain that —I'm not a male."

Forrester agreed silently. Diana was not a male. It was the most understated statement he had ever heard.

"But anyhow," Diana said, "they want wars, so they have wars. Mars sees that the wars stay small and keep within the Martian Conventions, though, so any really widespread damage or destruction, or any wanton attacks on civilians, are a thing of the past. And it's not only wars, kid. It's everything."

"What do you mean, everything?"

"Man needs a god, a personal god. When he doesn't have one ready to hand, he makes one up-and look at the havoc that has caused. A god of vengeance, a god who cheers you on to kill your enemies....You've studied history. Tell me about the gods of various nations. Tell me about Thor and Baal and the original bloodthirsty Yahweh. People *need* gods."

"Now wait a minute," Forrester objected. "The Chinese —"

"Oh, sure," Diana said. "There are exceptions. But you can't bank on the exceptions. If you want a reasonably safe, sane and happy humanity, then you'd better make sure your gods are not going to start screaming for war against the neighbors or against the infidels or against-well, against anybody and everybody. There's only one way to make sure, kid. We've found that way. We *are* the Gods."

Forrester digested that one slowly. "It sounds great, but it's pretty altruistic. And while I don't want to impugn anybody's motives, it does seem to me that —"

"That we ought to be getting something out of it ourselves, above and beyond the pure joy of helping humanity. Sure. You're perfectly right. And we *do* get something out of it."

"Like what?"

Diana grinned. She looked more like a tomboy than ever before. "Fun," she said. "And you know it. Don't tell me you didn't get a kick out of playing God at the Bacchanal."

"Well," Forrester confessed, "yes." He sighed. "And I guess that Bacchanal is going to be the one really high spot in a very shortened sort of life."

Diana sat upright. "What are you talking about?"

"What else would I be talking about? The Bacchanal. You know what happened. You must know-everybody must by now. Mars is probably demanding my head from Hera right now. Unless he's got more complicated ideas like taking me apart limb by limb. I remember he mentioned that."

Diana stood up and came over to Forrester. "Why would Mars do something like that and especially now? And what makes you think Hera would go along with him if he did?"

"Why not? Now that I've failed my tests —"

"*Failed?*" Diana cried. "You *haven't* failed!"

Forrester stood up shakily. "Of course I have. After what happened at the Bacchanal, I —"

"Don't pay any attention to that," Diana said. "Mars is a louse. Always has been, I hear. Nobody likes him. As a matter of fact, you've just passed your finals. The last test was to see if you could figure out who we were-and you've done that, haven't you?"

There was a long, taut silence.

Then Diana laughed. "Your face looks the way mine must have, over three thousand years ago!"

"What are you talking about?" Still dazed, he wasn't quite sure he had heard her rightly.

"When they told me the same thing. After the original Diana was killed in a 'hunting accident' —frankly, she seems to have been too independent to suit Hera-and I passed my own finals, I —"

She stopped.

"Now don't look at me like that," Diana said. "And pull yourself together, because we've got to get to the Final Investiture. But it's all true. I'm a substitute too."

CHAPTER 11

The Great God Dionysus, Lord of the Vine, Ruler of the Revels, Master of the Planting and the Harvest, Bestower of the Golden Touch, Overseer of the Poor, Comforter of the Worker and Patron of the Drunkard, sat silently in a cheap bar on Lower Third Avenue, New York, slowly imbibing his seventh brandy-and-soda. It tasted anything but satisfactory as it went down; he preferred vodka or even gin, but after all, he asked himself, if a God couldn't be loyal to his own products, then who could?

He was dressed in an inexpensive brown suit, and his face did not look like that of Dionysus, or even of William Forrester. Though neatly turned out, he looked a little like an out-of-work bookkeeper. But it was obvious that he hadn't been out of work for very long.

Hell of a note, he thought, *when a God has to skulk in some cheap bar just because some other God has it in for him.*

But that, unfortunately, was the way Mars was. It didn't matter to him that none of what happened had been Forrester's fault. In the first place, Forrester hadn't known that the girl at the Bacchanal had been Venus until it was much too late for apologies. In the second place, he hadn't even picked her; he'd kept his promise not to use his powers on the spinning figure of Mr. Bottle Symes. But Venus had made no such promise. Venus had rigged the game.

But try explaining that to Mars.

He didn't seem to mind what went on at the Revels of Aphrodite-being Goddess of Love was her line of work, and even Mars appeared to recognize that much. But he didn't like the idea of any extracurricular work, especially with other Gods. And if anything occurred, he, Mars, was sure damned well going to find out about it and see that something was done about it, yes, sir.

Forrester finished his drink and stared at the empty glass. It had all begun on the day of his Final Investiture, and he had gone through every event in memory, over and over. Why, he didn't know. But it was something to do while he hid.

It hadn't been anywhere near as simple as the Investiture he had gone through to become a demi-God. All fourteen of the other Gods had been there this time; a simple quorum wasn't enough. Pluto, with his dead-black, light-absorbent skin casting a shade of gloom about him, had slouched into the Court of the Gods, looking at everybody and everything with lackluster eyes. Poseidon/Neptune had come in more briskly, smelling of fish, his skin pale green and glistening wet, his fingers and toes webbed and his eyes bulging and wide. Phoebus Apollo had strolled in, looking authentically like a Greek God, face and figure unbelievably perfect, and a pleased, stupid smile spread all over his countenance. Hermes/Mercury, slim and wily, with a foxy face and quick movements, had slipped in silently. And all the others had been there, too. Mars looked grim, but when Forrester was formally proposed for Godhood, Mars made no objection.

The entire Pantheon had then gone single-file through a Veil of Heaven to a room Forrester just couldn't remember fully. At the time, his eyes simply refused to make sense out of the place. Now, of course, he understood why: it didn't really exist in the space-time framework he was used to. Instead, it was partially a four-dimensional pseudo-manifold superimposed on normal space. If not perfectly simple, at least the explanation made matters rational rather than supernatural. But, at the time, everything seemed to take place in a chaotic dream world where infinite distance and the space next to him seemed one and the same. He knew then why Diana had told him that the word "machine" could not describe the Gods' power source.

He had been seated there in the dream room. But it wasn't exactly sitting; every spatial configuration took on strange properties in that pseudo-space, and he seemed to float in a place that had neither dimension nor direction. The other Gods had all seemed to be sitting in front of him, all together and all at once-yet, at the same time, each had been separate and distinct from the others.

He wanted to close his eyes, but he had been warned against doing that. Grimly, he kept them open.

And then the indescribable began to happen. It was as though every nerve in his body had been indissolubly linked to the great source of God-power. It was pure, hellish torture, and at the same time it was the most exquisite pleasure he had ever known. He could not imagine how long it went on-but, eventually, it ended.

He was Dionysus/Bacchus.

And then it had been over, and a banquet had been held in his honor, a celebration for the new God. Everyone seemed to enjoy the occasion, and Forrester himself had been feeling pretty good until Mars, smiling a smile that only touched his lips and left his eyes as cold and hard as anything Forrester had ever seen, had come up to him and said softly:

"All right, Dionysus. You're a God now. I didn't touch you before because we needed you. And I don't intend to kill you now; replacements are too hard to find. I'm only going to beat you-to within an inch of your damned immortal life. Just remember that, buster."

And then, the smile still set on his face, he had turned and swaggered away.

Forrester had thought of Vulcan.

Mars wasn't a killer, in spite of his bully-boy tactics. He had too good a military mind to discipline a valuable man to death. But he was more than willing to go as near to that point as possible, if he thought it justified. And what he allowed as justification resided in a code all his own.

"Right" was what was good for Mars. "Wrong" was what disturbed him. That was the code, as simple, as black and white, as you could ask for. Vulcan was one of the results.

Vulcan had been Venus' lawful husband, as far as the laws of the Gods went. That didn't matter to Mars-when he wanted Venus. He had thrashed Vulcan, and the beating had left permanent damage.

The damage was translated into Vulcan's limp. Any God's ability to heal himself through the machine's power was dependent on the God's own mentality and outlook. And Vulcan had never been able to cure his limp; the psychic punishment had been too great.

Forrester ordered another drink and tried to think about something else. The prospect of a fight with Mars was sometimes a little too much for him to handle.

The drink arrived and he sipped at it vacantly, thinking back to Diana and her story of the Gods.

There was one hole in it —a hole big enough to toss Mount Olympus through, he realized. Where had the Gods gone for three thousand years? And how had they gotten to Earth in the first place?

Those two unanswered questions were enough to convince Forrester that, in spite of all he knew, and in spite of the way his new viewpoint had turned his universe upside down in a matter of hours, he still didn't have the whole story. He had to find it-even more so, now, as he began to realize that the human race deserved more than just the "security" and "happiness" that the Gods could give them. It deserved independence, and the chance to make or mar its own future. Protection was all very well for the infancy of a race, but man was growing up now. Man needed to make his own world.

The Gods had no place in that world, Forrester saw. He had to find the answers to all of his questions-and now he thought he knew a way to do it.

"Want another, buddy?"

The bartender's voice roused Forrester from his reverie. He had absent-mindedly finished brandy-and-soda number eight.

"Okay," Forrester said. "Sure." He handed the bartender a ten-dollar bill and got a kind of wry pleasure out of seeing the picture of Dionysus on its face. "Let's have another, but more brandy and less soda this time."

The drink was brought and he sipped at it, looking like any ordinary citizen taking on a small load, but tuned to every fluctuation in the energy levels around him, waiting.

Only a God, he knew, could hurt another God, and even then it took plenty of power to do it. Actually to kill a God required the combined efforts of more than one, under normal circumstances-though one, properly equipped and with some luck, could manage it. As far as his own situation was concerned, Forrester was prepared for a deadly assault from Mars. Maybe Mars didn't intend to kill him, but being maimed for centuries, like Vulcan, was nothing to look forward to, and it was just as well to be on the safe side. Just in case the God of War had managed to get one or two other Gods on his side, Forrester had talked to Diana and Venus, and had their agreement to step in on his side if things got rough, or if Mars tried to pull anything underhanded.

And any minute now....

Suddenly Forrester felt a disturbance in the energy flow around him. Somewhere behind him, invisible to the mortals who occupied the bar, a Veil of Heaven was beginning to form.

With a fraction of a second, Forrester was forming his own. But this time he took a little longer than he had before.

It wasn't the first time he'd had to run. For over a month now, he had been jumping from place to place, all over the world. He had gone to Hong Kong first. When Mars had traced him there and made a grab for him, Forrester had made a quick jump, via Veil, to Durban, South Africa. It had taken Mars all of forty-eight hours to find Forrester hiding in the native quarter, wearing the *persona* of a Negro laborer. But again Forrester had disappeared, this time reappearing in Lima, Peru.

And so it had gone for five full weeks, with Forrester keeping barely one jump ahead of the God of War.

And, in that month, he had achieved two important things.

First, he had begun to make Mars a little overconfident. By now Mars was fully convinced that Forrester was nothing but a coward, and he was absolutely certain that he could beat the newcomer easily, if he could only come to grips with him.

Second, Forrester had discovered that Mars' basic reflexes were a trifle slower than his own.

If Mars had been able to form his own Veil and step through it in time to sense the last fading glimmers of Forrester's Veil, he would have been able to follow immediately. Instead, he had to go to all the trouble of finding Forrester over and over again. That meant slower reflexes-and that, Forrester thought, might just give him the edge he needed.

But this time, Forrester was going to let Mars follow him-slow reflexes and all. This time, he waited that extra fraction of a second-and then stepped through the Veil.

He was in the middle of a great rain forest. Around him towered trees whose great trunks reached up to a leafy sky. The place was dark; little sunlight came through the roof of leaves and curling vines. A bird screamed somewhere in the distance, sounding like a lost soul in agony; the sound was repeated, and then there was silence.

Forrester was exactly where he had intended to be: in the middle of the Amazon jungle.

He had time for one look around. Then Mars stepped out of a shimmering Veil only yards away from where Forrester was standing. Immediately, Forrester felt Mars throw out a suppressor field that would keep him from forming another Veil. He did the same thing. Now, as long as both held their respective fields, neither could leave.

"Greetings," Forrester said.

The bird screamed again. Mars ignored it.

"You're just a little too slow," he said, grinning. "And now, buster, you're going to get it-and get it good."

"Who?" Forrester said. "Me?"

Mars hissed his breath in and fired a blast of blue-white energy that would have drilled through a foot of armor plate. But Forrester blocked it; the splatter of free energy struck at the nearby trees, sending them crashing to the ground. A small blaze started.

Forrester followed the blow with one of his own, but Mars parried quickly. A few more little fires began in the vicinity. Then Mars bellowed and charged.

By the time he reached the spot where Forrester had been, Forrester was fifty feet in the air, standing with his arms folded and looking down in an interested manner.

"You ought to watch out," he said. "You might stumble into a Venus Flycatcher down there. I mean besides the one you've got already."

Mars' mouth dropped open. He gave vent to an inarticulate roar of rage and leaped into the air. As he rose toward Forrester, the defender closed his eyes and changed shape. He became a rock and dropped. He bounced off Mars' rising forehead with a great noise.

Mars roared and dived for the stone-and found himself holding a large, angry tiger.

But an old trick like that didn't fool Mars. Tiger-Forrester, suddenly finding himself fighting with another tiger as ferocious as himself, began clawing and biting his way free in a frenzy of panic. He managed to make it just long enough to become a stone again, dropping toward the Earth.

For a moment, the other tiger seemed uncertain. Then, catching sight of the falling stone, he became an eagle, and went after it with a scream, claws outstretched and a glitter of hatred in the slitted eyes.

Forrester reached the ground first. The eagle braked madly, trying to escape a giant Kodiak bear. Forrester stood on his hind legs and battered the air with great, murderous paws. Mars scooted upward, already changing into something capable of coping with the bear. A huge, bat-winged dragon, breathing barrels of smoke, flapped in the air, looking all around for its opponent. It did not notice Forrester scurrying away in the shape of an ant through the leaves and thick humus of the jungle floor.

By now, the air was becoming smoky and the flames were licking up the sides of trees all through the vicinity, and racing along the giant vines that curled around them. The dragon belched more smoke, adding to the general confusion, and roared in a voice like thunder:

"Coward! Dionysus! Come out and fight!"

There was an instant of crackling silence.

Then Forrester stepped out from behind a blazing tree. He, too, was a dragon.

Mars snarled, breathed smoke and made a power dive. Forrester dodged and the fangs of the monster missed him by inches. Mars sank claw-deep into the ground, and Forrester slammed the War God on the side of his head with one mighty forepaw. Mars blew out a cloud of evil-smelling smoke and managed to jerk himself free. He leaped to all four feet, glaring at Forrester with great, bulging, hate-filled eyes.

"Man to man, you bastard!" he said in a flame-filled roar.

Forrester leaped back to avoid being scorched. He poured out some smoke of his own. Mars coughed.

"Damn it, no more shape-changing!" the War God thundered.

"Fair enough!" Forrester shouted. He changed back to his Dionysian form, circling warily until Mars had followed suit. Then the two began to close in slowly.

Around them the forest burned, vegetation even on the swampy ground catching fire as the entire vicinity crackled and hissed with heat. Neither of them seemed to take any notice of the fact.

Mars was a trained boxer and wrestler, Forrester knew. But it was probably a good many centuries since he'd had any real workouts, and Forrester was counting heavily on slowed-down reflexes. Those would give him a slight edge.

At any rate, he hoped so.

The circling ceased as Mars leaped forward suddenly and lashed out with a right to the jaw that could end the fight. But Forrester moved his head aside just in time and the fist glanced off his cheek. He staggered back just as Mars followed with a left jab to the belly.

Forrester clamped down on the War God's wrist and twisted violently, pulling Mars on past him. The War God, caught off balance, lunged forward, tripping over his own feet, and almost fell as he went by. Forrester, grinning savagely, brought his right hand down on the back of Mars' neck with a blow whose force would have killed an elephant outright.

Mars, however, was no mere elephant. He grunted and went down on his hands and knees, shaking his head groggily. But he wasn't out. Not quite.

Forrester doubled up his fist as Mars tried to rise, and came down again with all the force he could muster, squarely on his opponent's neck.

There was a satisfyingly loud crack, audible, even in the roar of the burning forest. Mars collapsed to the ground, smothering small fires beneath his bulk. Forrester leaped on top of him and grabbed his head, beard with one hand and hair with the other. He twisted and the War God screamed in agony. Forrester relaxed the pressure.

"All right, now," he said through clenched teeth. "Your neck's broken, and all I've got to do is twist enough to sever your spinal column. You'll be crippled for as long as Vulcan has-maybe longer."

Mars shrieked again. "I yield! I yield!"

Forrester held on. "Not just yet you don't," he said grimly. "I want some information, and I'm going to get it out of you if I have to wring them out vertebra by vertebra."

Mars tried to buck. Forrester twisted again and the War God subsided, breathing hard. At last he muttered: "What do you want to know?"

"Why did you and the other Gods leave Earth for three thousand years? And where did you come from in the first place? I want the *real* reason, chum." He applied a little pressure, just as a reminder.

"I'll tell you!" Mars screamed. "I'll tell you!"

And as the roaring flames crackled in the Amazon forest, the agonized Mars began to talk.

CHAPTER 12

Zeus, Venus, Diana and Forrester sat in the Court of the Gods, listening to a large, blue-skinned individual with bright red eyes and two long white fangs coming from a lipless mouth. The eyes were like a cat's, with slitted pupils, and the general expression on the individual's face was one of feral hatred and bestial madness. However, as he had explained, he was not responsible for the arrangement of his features. He was, he kept saying, only interested in the general welfare. What was more, it was his business to be interested. He was, as a matter of fact, a cop: Bor Mellistos, of the Interstellar Police.

"My rank," he had told them mildly, "is about the equivalent of your Detective Inspector."

"Technically," he was saying now, "you are all four guilty of being accessories-as I understand your local law phrases it. However —"

He smiled. It made him look unbelievably horrible. Forrester tried not to pay any attention to it.

"However," he went on, "in view of the fact that none of you could possibly have known that you were, in fact, accessories-that is, that you were dealing with a criminal group, if you understand me-plus the fact that Mr. Forrester, as soon as he did discover the facts, called us at once through the power machine —I feel that we can overlook your part in the matter."

Venus frowned. "Wait a minute. I'm not sure I understand this at all. What crime are the Gods supposed to have committed?"

"Not crime, miss," Bor Mellistos said. His eyes twinkled. Forrester gulped and turned away. "Crimes. Misuse of a neural power machine, for one-and the domination and enslavement of a less advanced intelligent culture for another. Both those are very serious crimes."

"Less advanced culture?" Forrester said. "You mean us?"

"I'm afraid so, sir," Bor Mellistos said. "You see, all the members of my culture are attuned to the power nodes of one neural machine or another, but this power is not meant to be misused. We have been searching for this group for a long time now."

"And you first got wind of them on Earth about three thousand years ago?"

"A little more than that, actually," Bor Mellistos said, "if you don't mind the correction."

"Not at all," Forrester said, looking at the fangs of the Detective Inspector.

"We were alerted after the radiations had been coming in for some time. The search for this group wasn't nearly as urgent then."

"And that's why they had to go into hiding?" Diana asked.

"Correct, miss," Bor Mellistos said. "The only one we managed to catch was the woman calling herself Aphrodite, or Venus." He looked at the substitute Venus. "That's the one you replaced, miss."

"How did you catch her?" Forrester pursued.

"Well," Bor Mellistos said, turning a faint shade of orange with embarrassment, "she was-ah-engaged in a secret liaison with a mortal at the time. Knowing that two of the other gentlemen would be furious with her if they discovered this fact —"

"Mars and Vulcan," Forrester supplied.

"Quite correct, sir," Bor Mellistos said. "Knowing, as I say, that they would be furious, she had taken special pains to hide herself. When the alarm reached the others that we were coming, they could not warn her. As a result, when she returned to Mount Olympus, we were waiting for her."

"Serves her right!" Zeus said with indignation.

Bor Mellistos said: "Quite," very politely.

"And then," Forrester said, "you patrolled this place for a while."

Bor Mellistos nodded. "We left about three hundred years ago, finally deciding that they had gone elsewhere. By the way, do you know where they were hiding all this time?"

"My guess," Diana said, "is that they were here on Earth, of course."

"Naturally, miss," Bor Mellistos said. "But where?"

Zeus shrugged. "All sorts of places. I ran a tailor shop myself, pressing and cleaning. I understand that Poseidon and Pluto entered freak shows-they were fine attractions, too. Pan lived mostly in the forests, doing well enough for himself running wild. Diana and Athena ran a small hairdressing studio in Queens. And Venus —"

"Please," Venus interrupted.

"Perfectly honorable profession," Zeus objected. "One of the oldest. Perhaps the very oldest. And I don't see why —"

"Please!" Venus insisted.

Zeus shut up with a little sigh.

"At any rate," Bor Mellistos said, "that's the story up to date. And now there's only the question of the Overseer positions. Would you like to fill them?"

"Who?" Venus asked. "*Us?*"

"Well," Bor Mellistos said, "you have the experience. And we do need someone to take over. You see, three thousand years ago your technical attainments were not large. There was little need for an Overseer. Now, however, you are nearly at the stage where you will be invited to join the Galactic Federation. And we must make sure you do not do any irreparable harm to yourselves during the next few years."

"Well," Forrester said, "how could we —"

"If you'll permit me, sir," Bor Mellistos said, "I can explain. You would work much as the so-called Gods did-but with no publicity, and a greater sense of responsibility, if you understand me. Earth would never know you were there."

"I'd have to-stay away from mortals?" Forrester asked.

"Exactly," Bor Mellistos said.

Well, Forrester thought, it had its compensations. In the three days that the Detective Inspector had been on Earth, Forrester had had time to think and to find out some things. Gerda, for instance, was getting married to Alvin Sherdlap. Forrester wondered what kind of love would let a woman choose a name like Gerda Sherdlap, and decided it was better not to think about it.

What did he have to go back to? History classes? Students? Even students like Maya Wilson?

Well, he was sure he could do better than that. He looked at Diana and became even surer.

"The remaining eleven Overseers," Bor Mellistos was saying, "will be along shortly. You will then be able to draw fully on the machine. You need merely follow world events and make sure that any-ah-regrettably *final* decisions are not made. Your actions will, of course, be very much undercover."

Forrester nodded. "This mass arrest of the Gods is going to cause an upheaval all by itself."

"Quite true, sir. But that will be worked out. I'm afraid I don't really know the details, but doubtless the other eleven who are coming will inform you more thoroughly on that score."

Forrester sighed. "About the Gods-what kind of punishment will they receive?"

"Well, sir," Bor Mellistos said, "it varies. Vulcan, for instance-the person who called himself Vulcan, or Hephaestus-will probably get off with a lighter sentence than the others. He was a mechanic, brought along under some duress to service the machine. But the sentences will be severe, you may be sure. Very severe."

Forrester didn't feel like asking any more questions about that. There was a pause. He looked at Diana again, and she looked back at him.

"Do you accept?" Bor Mellistos said.

Forrester and the others nodded.

Bor Mellistos said: "Very well. In that case, I will inform the other eleven Overseers already picked that they will be met by you here, on Mount Olympus, and that —"

But Forrester wasn't listening.

He had begun whistling, very softly.

The song he was whistling was Tenting Tonight.